T0124281

RIVER RUNS DEEP

Memoirs of a Tomboy

N ANCY W EISER

authorHOUSE®

AuthorHouse™
1663 Liberty Drive
Bloomington, IN 47403
www.authorhouse.com
Phone: 1 (800) 839-8640

© 2016 Nancy Weiser. All rights reserved.

No part of this book may be reproduced, stored in a retrieval system, or transmitted by any means without the written permission of the author.

Published by AuthorHouse 05/03/2016

ISBN: 978-1-5246-0676-3 (sc)
ISBN: 978-1-5246-0675-6 (e)

Print information available on the last page.

Any people depicted in stock imagery provided by Thinkstock are models, and such images are being used for illustrative purposes only. Certain stock imagery © Thinkstock.

This book is printed on acid-free paper.

Because of the dynamic nature of the Internet, any web addresses or links contained in this book may have changed since publication and may no longer be valid. The views expressed in this work are solely those of the author and do not necessarily reflect the views of the publisher, and the publisher hereby disclaims any responsibility for them.

Contents

RIVERS CURRENTS by nlweiser @7/15/2000

In my women's depth flows many currents.
One's a raging river, crashing against the rock
of time. Heedless of life's roaring waterfalls it
plummets to the rush of the sucking sea. The
rush itself is sought after to be tasted like a
fine wine and stir the quiet.

One current run's shyly, wrapped in a
morning mist. Its surface is mirror still,
reflecting, floating lazily in the sun. Dreamy
eyed it drifts in the breeze seeking quiet ponds
With lily pads in places where frogs croak and
cicadas rub legs.
As moonbeams lantern the current it contemplates the whys.
Always listening, it laps its waves on the shore
of life.

One current drifts in silted mud and dirty fish
guts.
It drags sluggishly through swamp fed bottoms.
Like a mud cat, it feeds on discarded garbage.
Fat and goggle-eyed it views the uselessness of
life.
Growing green with age it stinks of lost hopes
And grows purposeless with lack of sight.

One current is full of life. Diamond studded
andwave dancing
It dares the willow tips tease and the rapid's
passionate longings.

It courses through many channels. Some
are bedrock deep and pierce the heart with
poignant memories
Memories of fish egg beds, minnows well fed,
and a mother's delight flood times river.

Sometimes, as I slowly meander and fog drift,
I see driftwood dreams all sunken in sand.
And in
Mind's eye I fly with dragonfly wings to
beautiful heights.
One day soon I shall chart my course toward
the sea
As I float the ebb and ride the tide, baptized by
life.

Dedicated to the memory of my dear brother
Who like a star- burst illuminated my life.
Donald Beshers Parker

Sept. 1, 1937 R. I. P. April 30, 1997

1

Lay of the Land

River City's levee marks its boundaries.

At the southern end of the levee is a thriving shipyard where ironclads had been built during the Civil War. My girlfriend, Cathy, lives in a house with an iron roof just across from the shipyard. Cathy has the sweetest smile and a soft southern drawl. I can sit on her stoop and listen to her talk all day. I'm wearing my favorite grass stained old blue jeans with a short sleeved checkered shirt. Cathy has on her nicely pressed sundress and is barefooted.

"My great grandmaw Elsie got married at the tender age of 15," states Cathy proudly.

"Boy's are yucky. You won't catch me marrying at 15!" I say as I spit to the side to ward off bad luck.

"The girls back then all married young according to Granny Elsie. This is her house. She lived to be a 102. I remember sitting by her rocking chair as she told me stories. Seems she was afraid of the cannon balls being shot by the Confederates at the Yankee ironclads." Cathy then pretends to be Granny Elsie.

"Those dag-nabbit cannonballs would shoot past the shipyard and land smack dab in our front yard," Cathy said holding her nose to make a nasal granny voice. "My whipper snapper husband, aimin' to protect me, built me an ironclad roof for this here house. He was such a gosh darn romantic."

I laugh at Cathy's Granny imitation and pound the wooden porch in approval.

"Believe me when rain plink planks on our roof most people would say it can wake the dead. But to me it is like music to my ears and lulls me to sleep."

If it were me I'd keep a large supply of cotton balls handy so I could sleep on rainy nights. By the way. Have you seen the new mussel dredger at the northern end of the levee?" I ask.

"No I haven't. Have you?"

"Yes, and it looks just like a metal dinosaur to me. You know... the long neck kind called brontosaurs. But its a mussel eater not a plant eater."

"Where is it?"

"It's right next to the square, brick, two story Button Factory."

"Button, button whose got the button," chants Cathy acting silly as she twirls around in circles.

"I cross my fingers every time I go by the dredger to protect me from things that go bump in the night." I say as I giggle at her antics.

"You know you shouldn't walk under ladders or step on black cats tails either." admonishes Cathy.

"'Everybody knows that's bad luck. At least its bad luck for the black cat for sure." We laugh together over that one."

"And you know that if you step on a crack it will break your mother's back don't you?"

"Aw, I don't believe that one. I step on cracks all the time and Mom doesn't have a broken back." I change the subject quickly because the talk was getting kind of voodooish. "Do you know where the Ladoga Cannery is?"

"Of course I do, says Cathy. It's near the levee just off Main Street."

"Well my Aunt Thelma Ann works there now.

I wonder what a Ladoga is?" Wondering is what I do best.

"It sounds kind of Indian to me."

"Me too, but Native American is what my grandpa told me I should call Indians. Mom and Dad first meet pickin' peaches for that Ladoga Cannery.

"I didn't know your Mom was a peach picker. I thought only Mexican's did that." quizzed Cathy half disbelieving me.

"Oh yes, she says there's nothin' much worse than itchy peach fuzz down your back while pickin' under a merciless southern Illinois sun."

"Just thinking about it makes me itch."

"I wonder if its as bad as poison ivy?" I get terrible cases of poison ivy almost every summer.

"Doesn't old man Krane have a warehouse down at the north end of the levee too?"

"Yes, according to brother Jon E. its full of not only bales of hay but cotton too. When the feed corn crop is brought in its packed to the gills."

"How does Jon E. know whats in the warehouse?"

"Old man Krane's watchman got sick one time and he asked Jon E. to fill in."

"Jon E. is no way old enough to work a night shift!"

"I know that and you know that but I guess old man Krane didn't care a bugs-butt."

Cathy puts her hand to her mouth shocked I'd said the word butt. I kind of swagger when I say it trying to act tomboy tough.

'Don't you go babbling this to anyone but Jon E. almost died on that job." I warn Cathy.

"Oh my gosh. What happened?"

"He tripped crawling around on the top of the stacked bales of hay checking for hot spots and ended up hanging by one foot upside down all night long. His larynx was so swollen by the time they found him he almost chocked to death."

"Cross my heart and hope to die I won't blab a word. I didn't know compacted hay or corn gets hot spots."

"Guess they do. I wonder if compacted men and women get hot spots?" We giggle about that idea. Cathy's mom calls her in for lunch and invites me to stay. I politely decline and wander back home for my lunch. Sure wish I had a bicycle like brother. I know better than to ask for one for Christmas. We just don't have that kind of money. But it would be nice to zip right home. I'm hoping for a toasted cheese sandwich and tomato soup for lunch. Mom makes the best tomato soup from our home grown tomatoes. She's real careful about not letting the milk curdle.

2

The Flood

But I'm gettin' ahead of my story. Let's get back to the beginning. We had just moved into our new home on Lowell Street. Our small house on Main Street was too small for our growing family according to Mom. It was just one year after the Great Ohio River flood of 1937 that brother Jon E. was born. He was born in a rented room above a tavern according to mom. He's just a year and a half older than I am.

"How come Jon's middle name is E. Mama?" I ask as we eat supper. I know a lot of fancy folks call it dinner but we call it supper. First off we don't have a big dinning room. We eat in the kitchen.

"All the Sparks men have some form of Edward as a middle name. Ed, Edwin, Eddie, names like that. So we just gave him the letter E. for his middle name to be just a little different." declares Mom.

"It's different alright just like Jon E. himself," I say thinking of how weird my brainy brother is. "But hey, its tradition."

I love getting Mom and Dad talkin' about the great flood. I look at brother and he looks at me. Together we shout. "Tell us about the flood!" We do that sometimes. Say things at the same time. Its kind of spooky. We quick knock the table to chase away bad luck.

"Well in Cincinnati, Ohio the flood stage got up to 80 feet." declares Dad. "Do some calculating son. Telephone poles are around 35 feet high. How many telephone poles high would that be?" I think Dad is trying to make brother a math-a-me-ti-son.

"I'm guessin' its as high as two and a half telephone poles on top of each other!" declares Jon E. in wide-eyed wonder.

I think, "smart-ass" but sure don't say it out loud because I don't want my mouth washed out with soap. Believe me holding a bar of soap in your mouth because you've back talked or cursed is no fun. Dad then continues on with the telling.

"Even in River City it rose to 60 feet and our levees were not as high." I listen raptly because Daddy knows just about everything you need to know.

"That's pretty ding doggy high if you ask me!" I pipe up trying to sound just as smart as Jon E. but not succeeding.

"That's very true Pumpkin." says Dad as he gives me an encouraging pat on the head.

"When the levee broke we were evacuated by row boat to your Dad's sisters farm. As you know it's on high ground just outside of River City," chimes in Mom.

"We all survived on a bumper crop of yams," informs Dad.

"To this day I can't stand to eat yams. We had fried yams for breakfast, yam soup for lunch and baked yams with ham at night," informs Mom.

I can see why she was just plain yammed out.

"President Franklin D. Roosevelt sent thousands of WPA workers to the Ohio River Valley to distribute emergency food and housing to help the area's flood victims," recounts Dad.

"You were born a year and a half after the great flood of 19 37 and Jon E. just one year after." says Mom giving us both a kiss on the forehead as if to say at least something good came out of the flood.

"It's good seeing that major shipping has resumed on the mighty Ohio and Mississippi rivers." says Dad trying to sound positive.

"Your Grandpa Spears says you can stand on top of the new levee now and see towboats, sometimes called push-boats, with names like Big Al, Nancy Jo, and Tom Dewey chugging by." informs Mom. "They transport flatboats or barges laden with coal, cotton, grain and ore to different river town ports. The final port of call is New Orleans." informs Dad. The folks are always trying to "educate us".

Mom pats Dad on the hand and asks, "What's the river stage today Ben?"

"According the Karo Evening Citizen it's way below flood stage Hun. Nothing to worry about."

Checking the river stages is a way of life for the residents of River City. I guess once you've been in a flood the fear never goes away. I bet they check them real close in Cincinnati too! I just wonder. That's what I do best.

"Grandma Spears brought you over some prize buttons for your button collection today Lou Ann. You can look at them after supper. That is after you practice your piano."

I don't mind that order because I love practicing the piano. Especially since Mrs. Brody is now my teacher. I just love Mrs. Brody. She actually went to the Julliard School of Music. How she ever ended up in River City is beyond me. I wonder if it was love? I wonder about things like that a lot.

"Says here that Mr. Warner is going to be the prosecutor in the Hachet Annie case," Dad reads out loud. Mrs. Warner, his wife, was my first piano teacher. But I was so scared of going to the Warner mansion that sits upon a hill like a castle that I begged Mama to let me change teachers. I wonder if its sitting on top of an old Indian burial mound? That's what I do best is wonder. The Warner house looks just like a vampire's castle. No one

7

goes trick or treating at that house unless it's on a double dog dare. My wondering time over I get to practicing and time passes fast.

"I've practiced an hour Mom. Can I look at my buttons now?"

"Sure Pumpkin. I think there's even a Union Army button in the batch," informs Mom.

"I see it! It's silver and has an eagle with a body that's shaped like a shield." I quickly snatch it up and scotch tape it to my cardboard hall of button fame and label it. I have a wooden button that looks like a striped zebra skin right next to it. Most of my shoe box of buttons are made from the tons of plentiful mussel shells dredged up from the Ohio River's silt rich bottom. Many mussel shells are ugly as sin on the outside. Some mussel shells are as bumpy as an old horny toad. Some are smooth, and some flaky. Most are an ugly gravestone gray in color. But on the inside they are shimmering, pearly beauties.

"They look like a thin sheet of fresh water pearls," declares my ex-cheerleader Aunt, Aunt Julie Ann, who works in the button factory as a sorter and sometimes a stamper. Like my Mom is always saying. "You can't judge a book by its cover." I think she was talking about people but it sure does fit mussel shells too. I collect mussel shells, buttons and driftwood. If you live in a river town what else can a kid collect or do. Maybe collect donut holes or go snipe hunting. Dad settles into his favorite recliner chair to read the rest of the paper. No one but Dad ever sits in that chair. Its the man throne.

"It says here that the warehouse at the town's northern end is going to be declared a National monument," reads Dad out loud.

"Is that the one that is historically famous for having been converted into a hospital for Grant's troops during the Civil War of 1861." asks Jon E.

'There he goes again being a "smart-ass", I mumble under my breath.

"Yes, and son I'm proud of you for remembering that fact," Dad says as he pats him on the head. Jon E. is on the floor playing with his erector set. I think he's building a giant crane. It's either that or a dinosaur. I can't really tell the difference at this point.

I speak up and say, "They say it was a good place to die. They used old saws to cut off arms and legs for heavens sake!"

"Gory but true Lou Ann," says Mom. She had studied to be a nurse so she understood and totally agreed with what I was saying.

Receding flood waters at River City.

Dad and Mom pretending to drive Uncle Rory's
Model T at the Sparks family reunion.

3

Who is Kin to Whom

The last Sunday in August is here and we drive in Dad's pick up truck to the Spark's family reunion that's held every summer at the old homestead, which is just off the old river road. Mom sits primly by Dad in her Sunday best. Brother Jon E. and I get to sit in the bed of the truck.

"Keep your hands inside the truck bed and don't sit near the tailgate," warns Mom. "Don't forget how little Tommy Jones lost his arm sticking his hand out of a car window."

"It was such a tragedy," pipes up Dad. "Who could forget that. You obey your Mom you two and no horse'n around back there."

"Yes Mam" I say anxious to be on the way.

"Yes Sir," says Jon E. as he hops in the back of the truck and goes sit near the cab. Dad then lifts me up and sits me next to him. The speed of the drive makes my pigtails fly and cools us down. Its rip roaring hot so it feels good to feel the kiss of a breeze. We park in a swirl of dust near the old red homestead barn and Uncle Ed helps me out of the truck.

"Just in time for fried chicken," greets Aunt Mae Louise. The table is filled with country fare; yeast rolls, gravy, corn on the cob, fresh churned butter, snapped green beans with bacon, sweet peas, sliced juicy tomatoes, mashed potatoes and mounds of fried chicken. There was also a nice hickory smoked ham from the smoke house. All the Sparks family brothers, sisters and their spouses were packed around the big dinning room table. Jon E. and I were the only kids at the reunion besides our 3 older cousins; Aunt Mae Louise and Uncle Ed's children. A lot of 'please passin' is heard and then everyone gets down to the serious job of eatin'.

"I'm so stuffed I can't eat another bite," declares my extra large and loud mouthed traveling salesman uncle, Uncle Rory, as he pats his big belly.

"Lets all go sit on the side porch and let that wonderful meal digest," suggests my Uncle Rory's sweet tempered, shy wife Bessie.

"We have sun-tea or lemonade. You just sit and I'll fetch which ever you all want," volunteers Gracie the oldest Conner's daughter as we all tromp outside. The two-ton Spark family siblings with their spouses sit around the rap-around farm house porch in their Adirondack chairs, fanning themselves with cardboard church fans and talk endlessly about who is kin to whom. And I mean endlessly!

"You do know that Long John Dover just down the road from here in that one room shack is a distant kin don't you?" declares Aunt Mae Louise in her high pitched, delicate voice. Then she laughs as the kin folk get a shocked look on their face. When Aunt Mae Louise laughs it sounds just like tinkling bells. Makes me think of fairies dancing in a fairy ring and she smells just like lily's of the valley for some reason. I just love to hear Aunt Mae Louise's laugh.

"His great aunt married a Sparks after her first husband passed away." The Spark's kin all groan over this gem of information.

"That's not something I wanted to know. Long John is nothing but pure white trash. He's know for distilling pure grain whiskey that blinds folks foolish enough to drink it. Plus he beats his wife they say," declares my Dad.

"Get over it Ben. There's a skeleton in everyone's closet," pipes up Uncle Frank. Uncle Frank likes to tease. He likes to knuckle rub my head and declare, "Got me some carrot top luck now."

Grandma says I have auburn hair so I don't know why he calls me a carrot top. Maybe he's color blind?

"Who cares a bugs butt whose kin to whom," I whisper to brother Jon. "I'll knock Long John's teeth down his throat if he every tries to lay a hand on me. Never going to marry anyway. Especially not a feeble headed, country bumpkin like Long John."

Brother pokes me in the arm and covers his mouth to stifle a sputtering guffaw. We then grab croquet mallets to escape the adult's mind numbing genealogy babble and pile drive each others wooden balls across the dusty, dry country lawn. We don't bother to put up the wickets or the stakes. Jon E. has the stripes and I've got the solids. My Dad taught me how to pile drive. He was, at one time, the champion croquet player of Pulaski county.

"Pile drive" I yell as I hit Jon E.'s ball half way across the lawn. To pile drive you must put your ball next to the other ball then step on your ball so it won't move when you rare back with you croquet mallet and hit your ball so that it makes the other ball pile drive away.

"Pile drive" yells Jon E. as he tries to hit my ball even further. We did this until the cows came home and the fireflies announced dusk by flashing their tiny yellow-green taillights.

"Mosquito's are eating me alive," declares Uncle Frank as he windmills his arms trying to ward off the blood sucking pest.

"I swear they're big enough to carry off a feral cat this summer."

"Lets go in and have a supper snack then," offers Aunt Mae Louise. "There's left over yeast rolls and fried chicken. Gracie, go get a jar of that batch of mayonnaise you made that is so good and we can make sandwiches." Gracie is Aunt and Uncle Conner's oldest girl. She is the best square-dance caller in the county. She could win a hog hollering contest her voice is so strong.

"Who wants to crank the ice-cream maker?" offers Uncle Eddie Conners with a twinkle in his eye. Uncle Eddie has a peg leg but no one calls him 'Pegleg'. He lost his foot working as a brakeman for the railroad. He is well respected in the farm community.

"Me first" yell Jon E. and I at the same time. We then quick knock wood to ward off bad luck.

"You two can take five minute turns and when it gets too hard for you to turn you older kids take over," orders Uncle Ed as he points to his two other almost adult children. Zelma, his youngest, is movie star pretty and Joe, his middle child, is strong as an ox and built like one. Gracie, his oldest girl had helped Aunt Mae Louise make the fried chicken dinner so she was excused. Joe taunts us by saying "Come on kids put some muscle into it."

We set to the cranking like we were trying to win a prize at the county fair. Zelma cheers me on by saying, "Come on you can do it Lou Ann. Give it one more turn." I hang on trying to prove how tough I am but it finally got to much for me and Jon E. So they took over.

"What kind is it I ask," as I slobber like a rabid dog and lick my lips in anticipation.

"Fresh blackberry" states Zelma. "I was almost eaten alive by chiggers picking them yesterday. We went pawpaw pickin' up the road early this morning and I was hoping it would be pawpaw ice-cream but Maw said they weren't quite ripe enough."

"I've never seen a pawpaw. What do they look like and taste like?"

"They grow on a short tree with egg shaped leaves and look kind a like a long pear and kind a yellow-brownish in color when ripe. They taste kind a like a combination of banana and mango. But you can't eat the skin or the seeds," informs Zelma. "It will make you sick."

"Maw grinds the seeds into a powder and uses it to kill head lice which her students are always bringin' into the country school house," informs Joe.

"Want to know something gross Jon E?" asks Joe as he jabs Jon E. on the arm.

"Sure," I love gross."

"Well, the farmer who has the paw-paw patch at the edge of his cow pasture collects roadkill to put under the paw-paw trees to attract the carrion flies that pollinate the fruit. It sure makes it stinky pickin' paw-paws."

"That's for sure." chimes in Zelma holding her nose as if memory had a smell.

I find myself softly singing, "Pickin' up pawpaws put'num in a basket. Pickin' up pawpaws put'num in a basket. Pickin' up pawpaws put'num in a basket. Way down yonder in the pawpaw patch," as I wait for the ice cream to harden and a chance to lick the dasher. Being the youngest brother and I get to do the dasher lickin' honors. Our tongues almost freeze to the metal dasher it's so cold. The old folks then gather in the parlor with their bowls of ice cream and tell the story of how great grandfather, Captain Exavier Edward Sparks, of Grant's Calvary, had his leg cut off in Grant's hospital and near bleed to death. After that they called him Pegleg Sparks. My brother and I look at Civil War pictures on my daddy's sister, Aunt Mae Louise Sparks Conner's, stereoscope. The stereograph cards that go in the stereoscope have two duplicate images side by side with one slightly off center which makes the image seem to jump out at you. I love looking at the stereograph cards. My favorite bunch is the collection of famous Indian warriors photographs. They look so proud and fierce. In my minds eye I can see the warriors sneaking up on the farm. I'm glad I'm safe with family because Geronimo looks like he wants to reach out and scalp me. Really can't blame him. We white folk did steal all the Indian's land. One picture shows Indian women and children marching in a long line surrounded by soldiers.

"What's this picture all about Aunt Mae Louise?" I ask handing her the stereoscope. Aunt Mae Louise is a school teacher so I knew she would know.

"That picture is about the infamous "Trail of Tears." As she hands the stereoscope back to me you can see tears in her eyes.

"Many Indian baby's and elderly froze to death on that forced march. It was down right disgraceful in my option." Her voice cracks with emotion as she recounts the story. Aunt Mae Louise is a one room school teacher. That means she teaches grades 1 through 6 all together in one room. I wonder how she manages to do that? That's what I do best...wonder. It would be like teaching apples, oranges and bananas all at one time. She must be Superwoman! I giggle thinkin' of her in a cape wearing a sexy body suit, tights, and long boots.

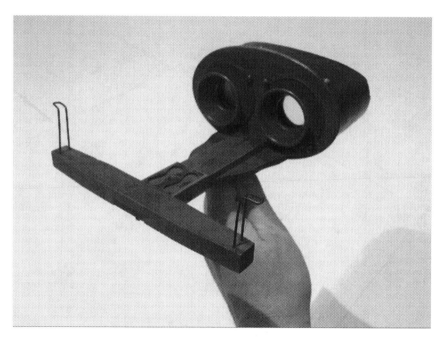

Aunt Mae Louise's Stereoscope.

Visiting Grandpa and Grandma Spears.

4

Mama's Side

My mom's side of the family was Scotch/Irish on her mother's side and French on her Dad's side. I even had a relative of my Grandma Spears that was named Annie Laurie Bell. We are staying a Grandma and Grandpa Spears house overnight because it is Pinochle Game night for Mom and Dad when that fact came up.

"You know that the lady in the love poem that the Scotch poet William Douglas wrote about is your kin don't you?" says Grandma as she unbraids my pigtails and combs out my hair.

"You mean Annie Laurie?"

"Yes, in fact I was named after her. So was one of my cousins." My one cousin even got her name changed so she could be an Annie Laurie."

Grandma Annie only had a third grade education but she could recite that poem from memory. I loved that poem. The rocking sing song of the poem would always put me to sleep.

"Put your jammies on and crawl into bed and I'll recite it for you."

I saw a tintype of her great aunt. She was a real beauty so I'm inclined to believe Grandma. Grandma's voice was almost a whisper as she recited...

"Maxwelton's brae are bonnie, Where early falls the dew" And "twas Bonnie Annie Laurie give me her promise true."

I think that's where I first got my love for poetry. Poetry just plain makes my heart sing.

"Jon E. you might be interested to know that your crazy Great Aunt Billie claims we are also kin to Thomas Jefferson."

"No way," pips up Jon E.

"I'm not kidding you. She says it is on the wife's side. "I read a book where it said Thomas Jefferson's brother-in-laws all had red hair like him." mused Jon E.

"Yes redheads run in the Epps branch of the family. So maybe its true." contemplates Grandma. Grandpa comes in and shoos us to bed.

"Now get yourself to bed you two. It's almost 9 o'clock." Grandpa then gives me a kiss on the forehead and pats brother on the head.

"Did you all brush your teeth and wash up good?" asks Grandma.

"Yes Mam!" we announce in unison and quickly knock on the wood bed frame.

As we lay under Grandma's homemade quilt I fall asleep thinking, Jon E. and I both have brownish red hair. That would be a prideful kinship if we truly are kin to Thomas Jefferson. I quickly fall asleep and dream about playing with redheaded cousins

"Rise and shine you sleepyheads," yells Grandma.

As we eat a breakfast of bacon, eggs and bisquets the next morning I kind of stare at Grandpa Spear's forehead. He has a bump that looks like a horn might burst out.

"Grandpa how did you get that bump in the middle of your forehead?" I ask.

"I've just always had it. Maybe I'm part unicorn he teases."

Grandpa is a tiny boned man of French ancestry. He's soft spoken and very shy but smart as a whip snake. I wonder why they call whip snakes smart? Is it because they can catch their tails? Sorry, got train wrecked there. Back on track to the Spears connection. I don't know why I didn't notice it last night but Grandma has blue hair. That usually means she has gone to the beauty shop and they put a rinse called White Minx on her pure white hair. It's supposed to take the yellow out of white hair but it just turns Grandma's hair a tinge of blue.

"Grandma how come you only have a 3rd grade education? I know you're just as smart as Grandpa and he graduated from high school.

"Thank you child for saying I'm smart. I've always regretted not being able to finish school. Unfortunately, I got jerked out of school when I was 9 years old because my Maw went blind. They needed me on the farm to do the cooking and sewing, washing, cleaning and gardening and to care of my Maw. My oldest sister was already married and living on a boxcar with her man who delivered mail by train. My middle sister, your Great Aunt Thelma was working in California and sending money home to help feed us."

"Wow! You did all that? When I grow up I want to be as strong as you! What caused your Maw to go blind Grandma? Was she in an accident?"

"No, she had diabetes and got Glaucoma which eventual blinded her."

"That is so sad. You aren't going to go blind are you Grandma? You have diabetes. I've seen you take your shots." I say with concern.

"No child. I'm very careful with what I eat and have my eyes checked regularly."

"Why are you so gussied up?" Are you going to go play Canasta?" I knew my grandma loved to play cards.

"No, I'm going to a Ladies Aide quilting party this afternoon." Do you want to come?" Grandma was always trying to get me to share her love of quilting.

"No thank you Grandma I'd rather go out and play. I'd rather do anything other than stick my fingers trying to hand stitch a quilt," I mumble to myself. As I finish breakfast I get to wondering how and why Grandpa and Grandma ever got together. As you know that's what I do best is wonder. I'll have to say I don't have a clue. My granddad was a barn painter when he was a young man. We actually have a black and white picture of him in his paint spattered overalls and white painters cap. He has a dripping white- wash brush in his hand, a shy smile on his face, and is standing in front of a large barn next to an old wooden ladder and a pail of white wash paint.. I wonder if that was Grandma's folks barn? It did say Tupalo, Mississippi on the back of the photograph. Grandma had said she was born in Mississippi. Grandma' s folks were farmers. I was listening behind closed doors and overheard that Great Grandpa was a drunk and sometimes beat them. The sun is out and I skip home to Mama just to ask her if she knew about Grandma's childhood.

"Yes, I do but I bet you didn't know that your Grandma ran away from home when she was 13 with a riverboat gambler."

"Why would she do that?"

"Your Grandma says as she got older it got to be dangerous to be around her dad. The gambler she feel for worked on the fancy showboat called 'The Goldenrod."

"That's a fancy name for a boat."

"Yes, and it was a fancy boat. I looked it up in a history book. The Goldenrod was considered the largest and finest showboat ever built being 200 feet long and 45 feet wide. She, showboats are named shes, had a seating of more than 1,400 people."

"Wow that sure is one big boat!"

"On the first night of marriage Grandma jumped ship and got the marriage annulled."

"What does annulled mean?"

"It means canceled out. She never has told anyone what happened. It must have been something really bad because your Grandma is a strong woman and can take almost anything."

Anyway, talk about opposites. According to Grandma Grandpa was very shy back then and still is if you ask me. I know if he is papering anyone's house he will walk all the way home rather than ask to use the owner's bathroom. Knowing my Grandma, who was 16 at the time they got hitched, she probably tracked him down, tackled and then hogtied him. Her laugh will make the rafters rattle. Maybe it was her smile that trapped him? According to her sister, Thelma, she was a beautiful young woman which probably helped in the trapping. I'll take all bets that she did the proposing. Just can't see Grandpa being brave enough to do the askin'. My name is Lou Ann. I'm a tomboy and this is my telling.

Grandpa Frankie painting the barn.

A once loving Jon E. with sister, Lu Ann.

5

Two Monkey's in the Family Tree

My brother is Jon (E.) Sparks. The E is a form of Edward. I call him a few other things besides Jon E. but I can't say them out loud because Mama would wash my mouth out with lye soap. Grandma heats and makes lye soap in a big black kettle in her backyard so we have plenty around... unfortunately. Jon E.'s classmates call him Sparkie. That's cause he's smart. He's a skinny boy that's all arms and legs. He has two crossed front teeth which makes him look a little like a squirrel. He also looks just like a spider monkey. He does have one big giant pumpkin sized head though. My Mom says his head was so big at birth he almost got stuck in the birthing canal. He still has a big head in more ways than one. He is the genius in the family and frequently reminds me I'm a "mental midget". I, unfortunately, do say stupid things... a lot. I'll never live down asking where East Virginia was. Hey, there is a West Virginia so why isn't there an East Virginia! Geography was never my strong point, as you can tell. But Jon E. calling me "Shit For Brains" is just plain mean. It's snapping turtle mean. Makes me see red. Makes me fightin' mad! Jon E. was a protective brother when I was a baby according to Mom but he sure has changed. He was born above a tavern and I think the tapped kegs fumes went straight to his pumpkin head brain. Sixteen months after his birth I came sliding out. I love hearing the story of my birth. Every birthday I ask for fried pork-chops with mashed potato's and brown gravy, corn on the cob and homemade biscuits for my special dinner and then beg them to tell me about my unusual birth.

"You popped out just like a purple grape", declares Mom.

"You were squallin' so loud you'd turned purple. We'd just moved to that tiny house near the old Grant's hospital site at the north end of town. Do you remember that house?" I nod yes because I do remember walking from that little white house to the vacant lot near us and playing house with a 4 year old boy named Mickie Paul on a slab of concert near the old hospital site. I would sweep the pretend slab floor with Mom's old broom and put dandelions in mason jars around the slab that I called my house to make it homey looking.

"Well, you were born in that little house and you came popping out prematurely in mid January."

"It was colder than a witches tit on that day." Dad reminisced.

"I was afraid to touch you being you were so small. I was afraid you would break. You were just a little over 5 lbs and looked just like a miniature "Betsy Wetsy" doll."

I give brother a threatening glare and he backs off calling me that nickname. He did snicker though so I showed him a knuckle sandwich just to make sure he got my message.

"You were so small I had to use hot water bottles packed around you in a dresser drawer as an incubator. I was so afraid you wouldn't live. But you were a fighter. And boy, oh boy did you have powerful lungs!" I smiled at that because I still have powerful lungs. You should hear my Tarzan yodel.

"Well I'm not breakable now. I'm a sure as tootin' rough and tumble tomboy, I'm as tough as an old horse hide. My parents smile when I say that and Jon E. just snickers again. We now live in a big, white, one story, wooden house in the middle of town on Lowell street. It has a front porch with a swing, and a big front window that looks into the front room. My parents bedroom is just beyond the sliding white painted doors that separate the front-room and their room. Those doors slide into the wall just like magic. We usually just leave the sliding doors open during the day. They slide them closed at night so neighbors don't see Dad walking around in his long underwear with a trap door and Mom in her long flannel night gown. Mom undresses in the closet so Dad won't see her naked. I wonder why she does that? They are married after all. I have my own private bedroom on the left side of the house and just beyond the bathroom my brother has his own private bedroom. No sleeping on bunk-beds in a small room anymore. Brother Jon E. snores like a freight train so I'm real happy about that. The kitchen with its pot bellied 'Warm Morning' coal stove is always stoked by my father early in the morning. As I said before, we don't have a fancy dining room. All our eatin' is in the kitchen. Behind the kitchen is an enclosed back-porch with lattice work walls. The white wringer washing machine and big metal rinse tub sits on the back porch. I once got my finger caught in that wringer helping Mom do the washing. I think they heard my scream all the way to Main Street. One time we had a pinball machine that Daddy was repairing sitting on the back porch. We got to play it free. That was fun. Dad adjusts and repairs one arm bandits for the owners of the Angle Inn. By adjust I mean he makes sure the odds are tipped to the owners likin'. Our house sits on a large lot right across from the grade school, and not far from the back levee. The Illinois Central Gulf railroad runs by our house. If I run alongside the caboose and wave hard they will throw me a giant piece of chalk. My Uncle works as a brakeman for them so they know me. Its great for marking out a hopscotch on our front sidewalk. Willa Mae, a girl just two houses down, and I love to play hopscotch together. Dad built us a picket fence to enclose our pecan trees. We have five pecan trees. Two of them sit outside the fence. One at the side of the house and one in the front of the house. As you can see we've come up in the world...at least house wise.

Velma Ann and the Spark's family monkeys.

6

Little Dreamer

I sit swinging in the front porch swing, being lazy and daydreaming my day away. I lean back and watch the fluffy clouds float by. One cloud looks just like a dog barking. I call those drifting clouds God's cotton candy pictures. To the right is a cloud that looks just like a dragon shooting fire. No wonder the dog is barking. I think the dragon just singed its tail. I smile to myself at the thought. It's a dazzling fall day and the bright, colorful leaves dance in the wind. A zephyr breeze makes the yellow leaves from the big pecan tree in the front yard rain down. My daydreaming swirls around the thought of a bumper crop of pecans this year. Most of the crop is still in their thick, green leather like husks just waiting for a frosty day and a big wind to pop up. Then the pecans will come raining down. I imagine squirrels wearing army helmets as they rush around gathering nuts. I giggle at the thought. The pecans are a major income for us and serve as our Christmas money. I get 50 whole cents for my help cracking and pickin' nuts. My Daddy made an awesome nut cracker so that we could help crack the pecans and get out the two nut meats inside completely whole. You get more money for the unbroken ones.. It has two long adjustable screw heads attached to a long board and a lever handle to pull them together when you put a soft shell pecan inside them. We have small soft shell pecans rather than the long hard shell variety. We also have two hand grip crackers besides this homemade big Bertha of a nut cracker. My two least favorite jobs in the pecan harvesting business are the hulling (that's the peeling off of the husk if any were still stubbornly hanging on. It stains your finger tips an ugly green. Had to use grandma's homemade lye soap to get them clean last year.. I also hate to use the tiny, thin, sharp pointed pecan pick to get out broken tidbits. I've thought about using Grandma's quilting thimble to protect my sore fingers when picking but she would wallop me good if she caught me using her precious thimble. There is a candy company in Mounds, MO. who loves our tasty, small, paper shell pecans. Many people chunk our trees in the fall. Dad doesn't mind them getting the fallen pecans outside the fence but many a chunk of wood ends up on our roof and has come close to breaking a window. Its not just kids doing the chunk in' either. I've seen grown ups throwing at the hanging pecans too. It's a sight to see my dad racing out the back door like a small enraged bull screaming at the chunkers. When the crop looks like its ready we hire men to cover the yard with tarps, They climb up into the trees and shake the limbs until all the ripe pecans fall down. Brother and I have the job of gathering the fallen pecans outside the fence line. Of course we are in competition with every able bodied adult and child in the town for this nut gathering frenzy. Nothing is tastier than pecans roasted in a tin can in a leaf burning pile. Its a reward for the raking. Of course you sometimes do have to duck the projectiles of hot exploding pecans as they shoot out of the can. But believe me they are um um good!

I sit idly swinging and musing over what the Congregational minister said last Sunday.

He'd said, "We are brother and sister to all living things."

Did that mean I was kin to the big Catalpa tree at the corner of our street? Was I kin to the hummingbird who was fluttering around the honeysuckle bush behind me? I pull off one of the honeysuckles and bite off the end to suck up its sweetness. I pretend it's fairy wine. I nod to my sister hummingbird as we share this tiny drink. I wonder if the long Catalpa pods hanging down on the corner tree are Catalpa babies? I don't dare ask anyone. They will just laugh at me; especially brother Jon E... But I do wonder. Wondering is what I do best. I hope the preacher asks the congregation to sing, "In the Garden" this Sunday. I love that song. Mom is in the kitchen fixing supper. I hear music on the radio and her humming a Glen Miller tune called, "In the Mood". She bangs the pots and pans with a wooden spoon to the jazzy beat. Mom and Dad love to dance. They go to a place called the Purple Cackle on Sat. nights when there's a dance band on the bill. Sounds like a witch's den to me. We get to stay with Grandma and Grandpa Spears on those nights. I love to play with Grandma's collection of small ceramic figurines. My favorites are her spotted lamb, an oriole bird, and three tiny little wiener dogs. It's almost dusk and I sit swinging in the front porch swing waiting for my Daddy to get home. My five year old legs are too short to reach the porch so I pump it back and forth by throwing my chubby body to and fro. My auburn curls bounce freely around my head. I'm bored, hot, and restless. I want my Daddy. He always treats me like his little princess and he definitely is my knight in shining armor.

"Lou Ann, it's time for your Dad's bus to get in. Why don't you run up town and go surprise him with a walk home together?" yells Mom from the kitchen.

"May I Mom, really. All by myself?"

"Take Whiskers with you if you need company."

"I don't need company but I bet Whiskers would like a walk. I'd better rope her so she won't chase squirrels though." Actually I was a little scared of going by myself but would never admit it to anyone. Whiskers was a mixed breed stray that looked like a short four legged mangled hair brush with scruffy gray/ white bristles. She had the cutest bushy eyebrows though and a really cute, short wiggly tail.

"Good idea. Now scoot. The bus from Rational City is due in five minutes."

I run all the way to the bus stop dragging Whiskers along on a clothes line rope leash. We arrived just as the bus pulls in. You could hear the release of its air brakes a block away. As I run into the arms of my Daddy I hear the unwelcome, gravelly voice of old man Hager. Mr. Hager looks like a pug faced boxer and I don't mean the two legged kind. He always has the stub of a stogie in his mouth and talks around it. I scrunch up my nose for he smells of stale smoke and old whiskey. Dad sometimes worked for him fixing things. Dad can fix anything.

"Hey Fats, how's the number crunching business?" You could just hear the sneer in his voice. Old man Hager never got past eighth grade and hated anyone who had and that meant my Daddy.

Daddy just turned politely around and said, "Just fine Bo.. Just fine. By the end of the year I'll have that accountant degree and things should look up. And how's the Mom & Pop business doing?" Old man Hager made big bucks by carrying the tabs of poor blacks and whites at his crummy excuse for a grocery store and charging them double for doing so. My Dad said they owed their soul to his grocery store. It was their bought and paid for votes that put Old man Hager in as mayor of River City. I know my folks sure didn't vote for him.

"Making money hand over heels Fats. You should try it sometime." I wanted to punch old man Hager's lights out for mean mouthing my Daddy. But, of course I was just a little kid so I just scowled my meanest scowl at him and pretended I was Superwoman and could sizzle him with my x-ray vision.

My gentle, soft spoken dad, Ben E. Sparks, works at the shipyard in River City on weekends and the lumberyard in nearby Rational City during the week. He is studying a mail order correspondence course to become a certified accountant. My Daddy is smart. He even had a year of college. He dropped out when the college required that you must learn to swim, My Dad is terrified of deep water. His two older brothers had thrown him in a pond when he was just 4 to teach him to swim and he had gone straight to the bottom. They had to drag him out and pump out his belly. That's why he's afraid of water. Daddy is a hard worker. So we never go hungry in spite of the fact that times are tough for everyone in River City.

Tomboy and Daddy's little Princess Lu Ann dreaming the day away.

7

Around The Knight's Table

"We're home Sweetheart. What's for supper?" yells Dad, as we enter the lattice enclosed back porch. Dad takes off his sawdust covered overalls and his dirt clogged shoes so he won't mess up Mom's spic and span mopped kitchen. My mom, Velma Ann, who is 5' 8" to my dad's 5' 5"" was called 'Slim the Slop Eater' in high school by the mean kids and just 'Slim' by her friends. As you may notice southern towns are rattlesnake mean when it comes to nicknames. My parents look like the cartoon characters Mutt and Jeff standing next to each other. He was the short stubby Mutt and she was the tall thin Jeff. Mom could have been a model. She was so thin and moved so gracefully. She had almost a years study of nursing. People were always coming to her and asking her what to do when someone was sick. She usually knew what to tell them too. She got a gum disease called (pie oh re a) or something like that, and had to drop out of nursing. Too bad she got sick before she finished. She would have made a great nurse. My Mom was also the best cook in the county. Well, maybe second best.

My Grandma Spears cooked the best fried chicken in all of Illinois, maybe the whole world!

"I made fried pork chops and mashed potato's, and gravy and of course cornbread. ...one of your favorite dishes Love." My mouth drooled at those words. My Dad and I both loved fried pork chops. I always ordered it for my birthday dinner.

"Lordy, lordy Sweetheart, I think I died and went to heaven. "With those words he grabs Mom around the waist and draws her in for a big hug and kiss. My parents were very open about their love for one another. It was down right embarrassing to watch.

"Oh Mama and Papa, do you have to be so yucky?"

Mom just smiles and says, "Lou Ann, kissing is not yucky. Just wait until you're a young lady and find yourself a nice beau. You'll see what I mean. And what's this I hear about you popping Bobby Joe in the nose and making it bleed. His mom came over and chewed me out for letting you get by with (dressing like a hooligan and acting like a heathen) as she put it."

"He called me Loopy Lou. No one gives me a mean nickname and gets by with it. He was lucky I didn't beat him to a pulp," I mumble in defense. After all I had the reputation of being a rough n' tumble tom-boy to live up to.

Mom surprised me by winking at Dad and saying,

"Well, just don't hit him in the nose again. Aim for his arm if he persists in being so ungentlemanly."

"Yes Mam," I gulp in surprise and relief. Changing the subject as quickly as I can I say,

"Is Aunt Julie Ann coming to supper tonight?" I was hopeful because she often brought me unusual buttons for my button collection. I had a whole shoe box full of some prize buttons. Grandma gave me buttons for my collection too. My youngest Aunt, Julie Ann, works at the Button factory. They dredge the river bottom near by and use the mussel shells to make the buttons. You know the inside of a mussel shell is pearly white don't you? Aunt Julie Ann had just graduated from High School and this was her first job. She had been a cheerleader in high school. She made life bubble. She made everyone bubble. She was almost young enough to be my older sister. In fact she was young enough to be my Aunt Ruby's daughter instead of my Grandmother's daughter. That always made me wonder. But as you know wondering is what I do best.

"Yes, she is coming to supper. She said she had a surprise for us."

"For me or for us" You sure she didn't say for me?"

"No Lady Bug, she said for us. My mom called me Lady Bug and my dad called me Pumpkin as terms of endearment. I didn't mind those nicknames. They made me feel kind of fuzzy warm inside.

"Is Aunt Thelma Ann coming to supper too?" Aunt Thelma Ann worked at the Cannery and sometimes brought us the dented tin cans of peaches they were going to throw out. Visions of peach cobbler danced in my head. My Mom says I have a sweet tooth a mile long.

"No, she is eating at your Grandma and Grandpa's place. She said something about wanting to write to her soldier boy before bed. You know Benny I think she's very seriously in love with this soldier boy. She has been talking about moving to California just to be near him."

"He is a nice young man Sweetheart. He is very shy and I hardly got a word out of him when he was down for a visit while he was on leave, but it was obvious he was head over heels in love with our Thelma Ann."

It's a southern tradition to use both first and middle names when addressing friends. It was a family tradition for every girl's middle name to be Ann in honor of my Great Grandmother, Annie Laurie Bell. She was supposedly a great beauty as a young woman and to even have had a poem written about her.

"Where is Aunt Ruby Ann eating mom?" Aunt Ruby Ann worked at the courthouse for a very handsome lawyer. She was the beauty of the Spears family. I still live in the glow of having over heard one of Mom's friend's say I looked just like my Aunt Ruby Ann. I knew it wasn't true but I lived for weeks in the glow of that second hand glory.

"She said she had to work late again tonight. That's the fifth time this week she has given that excuse. I'm worried about her Ben. You don't think there is any hanky- panky going on do you? Her boss has a reputation of being a ladies man. Even though he's a married man."

"What's hanky- panky mom?"

"Never you mind Lady Bug. Small jugs sure have big handles don't they", she said as she winked at Dad. "You go set the table for five Lou Ann and I'll finish up the gravy. Then you can go practice your piano a little before supper. Your brother should already be home from his paper route. He sure is running late," said Mom with a worried scowl on her face.

I didn't tell on him but I knew he planned on stopping at Reatha's florist's shop to shoot the breeze. She always gave him a cool glass of lemonade. Reatha Mayberry was one of the few black business owners in River City. She was pretty too. As pretty as a sunflower in June.

"You'll have time to read your paper Ben. Jon E. and Julie Ann should be here shortly."

"Think I'll do just that." Dad's favorite chair in the living room creaked as he sat down and you could hear the rustle of the newspaper as he scanned the Karo Evening Citizen. Nobody ever sat in Daddy's chair. It was like his throne. My brother, Jon E., earned fifty cents a week for delivering each paper. He delivered to the whole town. He gave me a nickel a week to help him fold them into star shape so he could toss them from his bicycle right onto a subscriber's porch. He gave me another nickel when I helped him collect on Saturdays. He promised I could help him deliver when I got old enough to ride a bike. First I would have to get a bike and they didn't grow on trees.

"It says here that Grant Valley got the job of sheriff' s deputy", my Dad quotes from the newspaper.

"It's about time a black man got a decent job in this town. He's as big as a Mac Truck so he'll not have any trouble keeping order," declares Dad.

"He probably got it because he is the biggest, meanest looking buck around and Bo thinks he can keep the other blacks in line."

"Why'd you call Mr. Valley a buck, mama? Isn't a buck a male deer?"

"Never you mind Lou Ann. Just forget I said that," said Mom a little shame faced. "And don't go repeating it unless you want a whipping"

Dad frowned and said, "Sad but true my love but you know he really doesn't have a mean bone in his body."

"I know hon. I know. It's all in appearances."

My folks were hard working, church going, and kind to even the rail riding bums that came knocking at our back door for hand outs. My brother, Jon E., says there's a mark on our back fence that lets the bums know we're suckers.

"Papa, what do Charlie Boy & Easter Baby's parents do for a living? I often see them leave the house with lunch pails really early and they don't come back until really late."

"Whatever work they can find to survive hon. You see, Pumpkin, blacks in River City, often work like dogs and didn't get paid squat. Most are poorer than church mice. But never forget they are good, hardworking people. Most are honest but humble to a fault. Life is no bowl of cherries for them. Did I tell you, Velma Ann, I saw Charlie and Easter picking cotton down by the back levy in the heat of midday yesterday? I swear it was 110 degrees in the shade yesterday! That's disgraceful making anyone, let alone kids, work in that heat. I bet that's Hog Plover's patch of cotton. He tries to squeeze juice out of a turnip. He's a red neck of the worst kind too. Lazy as sin himself, but works his farm hands like they're dogs. He must weigh all of 300 pounds. "My respect for Charlie Boy and Easter Baby shot up ten fold. I knew I would have passed out from hoeing cotton in that heat.

"I believe their mom, Reva Jones, works for Widow Greaves doing house cleaning. Widow Greaves is as mean as a polecat. I saw her beat her old dog last week just because he was barking at the milk man. That heavy hickory cane of hers nearly broke the poor things back. I know it wasn't any of my business but I yelled at her. I don't like to speak ill of anyone but that was cruel and uncalled for. The preacher would starve to death if it was up to Widow Greaves. Her idea of tithing is thumpin' the bottom of the collection plate as its passed! So you can bet your bottom dollar that Reva Jones isn't getting paid squat."

"I saw old Joe Jones digging ditches for the city last week, chimed in Dad. Did you know they're trying to put in sewer lines on Main Street now? They have to dig shallow because the water level is so high with the river being so doggone close. Charlie and Easter's parents are just scratching for a living like the rest of us. But knowing the Mayor, I'm sure old Joe, being a black man, was paid way below minimum wage."

"That's not fair Daddy."

"Very true Pumpkin. Very true. But life often isn't fair. Now quit stalling and start practicing your piano like your Mom told you." I like practicing so I did run through my lesson for almost a half hour before Jon E and Aunt Julie Ann get home. As we sat down for supper, Aunt Julie Ann did have a surprise for us. And it was a whooper! She showed us an engagement ring! I didn't even know she had a beau. She said his name was Paulie and that he earned good money as a barber. She showed me a picture of him and I think I'm in love. He has the most gorgeous golden hair I've ever seen. He looks just like Prince Charming in the fairy tale books. She also told us she was taking instructions in the Catholic faith. I didn't know you had to go to school to be a Catholic. I wonder why you have to do that? We are all different religions in our family so it was no big deal to be Catholic. Two of my best girlfriends are Catholic. There's a lot of kneeling and crossing in that religion. My Grandmother is Baptist. They shout a lot. My family is Congregationalist and we sing a lot. My Grandfather says he's a Christian and does his praying private like and at home. All the sudden I hear Dad and Jon E. get into an argument over the gestation period of an elephant. How in the world that conversation came up I have no idea. Our bible of knowledge is the Encyclopedia Britannica. So out it comes and believe it or not Jon E. won. Me, I like to look at the pictures in the encyclopedia. Especially the illustrations of the insides of the body. Jon E and Dad actually read the darn books. Aunt Julia Ann honors me by asking me if I would pass out programs for her wedding. Mom promises to make me a dark blue velvet skirt and vest for Julia Ann's wedding which will be next August I can hardly wait! I've never had anything made out of velvet!

Jon E., paperboy, with Whisker's the dog.

DUST BROWN DAYS

By NLWeiser 1965

The paddle-wheel of a threshing machine
Floats through an ocean of grain.
And in its wake a swath is cut
That perfumes the goldenrod day.

The sweet hay smell of country air
Fans memories of dust-brown days.
Days when the young shout "Double dog dares"
Then swing from the loft In wild "Tarzan" play.

Those childhood days of simple fun,
Race swifter than swallows in flight.
My dust-brown days are too far a run
For my hair has turned quite gray.

But I'll run the sun, when memory comes,
With the smell of fresh mown hay......

8

Me Tarzan you Jane

My dust brown days were slowly coming to an end and my first day at school was approaching. My brother and I had just come back from our summer stay with my Aunt and Uncle Conners on the farm. This year there had been a hay gathering. The ladies all made a picnic like outdoor lunch and the men all helped with the haying. That's how they do things in farm country. They help each other. I think its kind of nice. We kids got to swing from the barn loft and drop into the piled hay. Little Jimmy Pickin's almost broke his arm when he missed the deep part of the hay. His older sister should never have let him try such a big kid game.

"Mom, can I go out and play with Charlie Boy and Easter Baby a little bit before bedtime?" Charlie Boy' s twin sister was Easter Baby. She was frail and very shy. Easter Baby always covered her mouth when she smiled. It was as if she believed that showing happiness was tempting fate. They lived directly behind us on Jewel Street. Jewel Street was like a demarcation point. Blacks lived on that street or behind it in the run down, slum houses.

All the whites, even the extremely poor ones, lived in much better houses in the city proper. Except for the poor whites that lived in the mayor, Bo Hager's, slum subdivision behind the back levee. There was only one black family I knew of that didn't live on Jewel Street. They were a rich family that owned a furniture store. They were honey colored blacks and a very handsome family. All the children were older so I didn't really know them.

"Sure Lady Bug. But don't stay out too long or the mosquitoes will carry you off for a picnic snack."

"We just want to catch fireflies and make firefly lanterns. Do you have any mason jars we can use?"

"Sure ladybug. Just let me poke a few holes in the lids with the ice pick and you'll be all set. I'll make one for each of you."

"Thanks Mom" I say but shyly withhold a deserved hug. After all I had a tough, tom-boy image to preserve in front of my friends.

"Stay just outside the backyard fence so you can hear me when I call you to come in." For some strange reason I can never get the twin's to come inside our fence and play in my backyard. It was like it was out of bounds for them. During the day we play things like kick the can, stick ball, or play act Tarzan. I always play hard from dawn to dusk with nary a worry about safety. We live close to the grade school play ground which has a jungle gym, monkey bars, whirling swings and a basketball court you can play on outside. The grounds were covered with white chat so falling down is not a good option. My favorite game is play acting "Tarzan" movies on the grade school lot. I always call first dibs at playing the part of Tarzan. After all I am a tomboy and can swing on the monkey bars like an Ape Man better than anyone "Me Tarzan, you Jane, come Cheetah." I say. Sometimes I like to play the part of Cheetah too as I hang upside down on the jungle gym grunting "Hoo, Hoo, Hoo". Charlie Boy likes to act the part of a native chief. He thumps his chest, shouts "Ugh" and pretends to throw a spear at charging lions. Easter always plays Jane, which I consider the wimpiest character. But she likes playing the girl part. "Go figure." I was crawling around on top of the monkey bars one day and slipped between them. I was terrified I was going to drop and break my arm and hung on deperately. Lumps older brothers were playing basketball on the outside court and heard me scream.

"Just drop stupid. Your not going to kill yourself," sneered the oldest brother. "Give her some slack, Leo can't you see she's terrified. Here you go little one. I'll just hold you by your waist and you can drop. I won't let you get hurt." I did as he told me and he gently placed me on the ground. It had only been a few feet down but my imagination had made it seem a mile away. I was so embarrassed by my untomboy like behavior. I wanted to run and hide. But I thanked my savior, snarled at his brother, and walked shakily away wiping my tears..

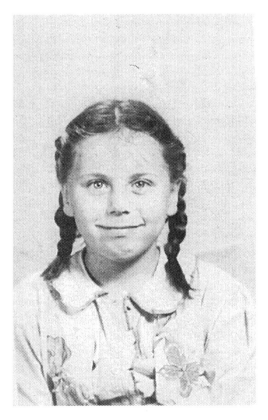

Me Tarzan you Jane.

9

Just Not Fair

The lazy years of early childhood passed slowly. But finally the fall of 1946 loomed into being. I was so excited about getting to go to school. My birthday was such that I was going in as one of the oldest in my class. I was a gangly girl built like a small bulldog. Mom platted my hair into pigtails as I chattered excitedly about going to first grade.

"Will they teach me to read Mama? Will I make any friends?"

"Yes, Lady Bug. If you work hard in school you'll learn to read and if you are friendly yourself you will make friends."

"Will Charlie Boy and Easter Baby be in my class?"

Maw took a deep breath and took a long time to answer and I looked at her quizzically noting her strange behavior. In a voice that was unusual tight she said,

"No Honey. But first let me tell you to stop calling Charlie "boy" and calling Easter "baby". That is not their names and its demeaning. You're a big girl now, and so are they."

"I thought that was their real names Mama. I would never demean them, whatever that is.

"Demeaning is deliberately trying to make a person feel worthless." And no, they won't be in your class."

I looked at Papa in disbelieve.

"But they're the same age as I am. Why won't they be in my class?"

Papa had not left for work yet and he added in a shameful whisper, "Blacks aren't allowed to attend "white" schools Lou Ann. They have to go to their own school." informs Papa.

"They have their own school?" Where is it? What is it named?"

"Its not far from the County Courthouse," he informs me.

"Its named after an abolishinest of Abraham Lincoln's day named Elijah Lovejoy."

"I don't even know what an abolishinest is. But I know it's not fair to seperate us just because we're different colors," I scream near tears from anger. Charlie and Easter should be in my class. They're my friends!"

"No, it isn't fair. Maybe one day we can change that. But right now that's just how it is", said Papa.

Mom added, "We're close to the Mason-Dixon line. Almost deep south. What do you expect."

Jon E. pipes up with, "You'd think we lost the Civil War instead of winning it. You're right for once Lou Ann. It isn't even close to fair."

At the evening meal my parents ask how my first day at school had gone.

I hang my head and mumble, "I feel out of my chair while testing the chair's balance. It sure made a loud crash."

"Did you get a whipping. from the new first grade teacher, Miss Fay?" Jon E. asks hopefully.

"No, I say sticking my tongue out at him," I just had to stand at the chalk board with my nose in a circle for five minutes"

"Well, Dad said laughing out loud, I guess you won't be rocking in your chair anymore."

"No Sir. I sure won't," I grin relieved he wasn't disappointed in me. I was Daddy's girl and would rather die than displease him. As we made a desert of cornbread and molasses, Dad talks about his first school board meeting.

"This is just between the family and mustn't be spread about. I just found out that the "black" schools are getting nothing but "white" schools discards. Old books with no covers and pages missing."

"That's not fair Papa. Not even close to fair," yelled brother Jon.

"Not only that it's got to be against the law. I'm going to try and put a stop to that. Such doings are a sin and disgrace to man and God." The passion in his normally quiet voice was shocking to all of us. "And yes, Lou Ann and Jon E. You are so right! It just Isn't fair!. One of these days I may be shot for proposing it. But the new grade school principle is on my side and we are making plans for a vote of consolidation. It only makes sense. Both schools would be better off if they would just merge."

The years passed slowly and without much excitement. I never played with Easter any more. It was like she was a ghost and we could see straight through each other. Charlie would still play stick ball with me at the side of the house but he wouldn't go on the grade school playground anymore. It was like he was afraid now. I could understand why. Even my brother was chased on the playground and sometimes beaten up by Red Cazwell and his gang of back levee thugs. Red had to come to first grade in overalls with no shirt and tennis shoes with holes in them. He didn't have any socks. I guess living that poor would make anyone pretty mean. He is definitely the school bully and a real back levee red neck. He even makes my ears burn when he lets out a line of cussin'. He turns the air blue with all that @#$#@ he yells at you. I wouldn't be surprised to see him spit tobacco one of these days! No telling what they would do to a black boy like Charlie if they caught him on "their" territory. As Mom says, "We are awfully close to the Mason-Dixon line." I think that means the Civil War really hasn't ended around here at least freedom wise for the blacks. I'm pretty sure I'm right about that. I don't even have to wonder.

10

Dust Brown Days

I was going to be in the 3rd grade this fall and loved to read. I'm such an avid reader I think the town council thought since I almost lived at the library during the summer I might as well work there. So I gladly took the offered volunteer job of town librarian. Our town library was housed below the small bandstand on Main Street. It looks like an enclosed gazebo. I just love the musty smell of old books and I judge my books by their size. The bigger the better. Right now I'm reading "Swiss Family Robinson" and loving it. It weighs at least a pound so it's no wimp book. My Mom loves to read too. She likes to read love stories. You really get an insight into people from what they checkout to read.

On weekends I love to wander the front levee hours on end looking for interesting driftwood. Some times I take my scruffy looking dog Whiskers along for company. Mom and Dad don't know it but Jon E. sneaks Whiskers in at night and sleeps with him. But he's my dog too and likes to wander with me. It's a blistering hot day today. It's a "you can fry an egg on the sidewalk day". I spot one driftwood's white, sun bleached shape that reminds me of people's twisted arms reaching for the sun. "Look at that one Whiskers. I bet it'll clean up real good." Whiskers wags her tail in agreement so in my gunny sack it goes and off I go searching for another interesting piece. I find a small, beautifully grained piece and stick it in my sack. I wonder if its a piece of cypress wood? Its almost red enough to be cedar. I'll check it out more when its cleaned up. I spot a bleached piece of wood that looks like a curved bread basket and have to dig it out of the sand with my hands. It looks like it may be oak. The smell of dead, washed up Gar along the levee was beginning to make me gag. A Gar is the ugliest fish I've ever seen. It's even uglier than a catfish! It's torpedo shaped with silver, slimy scales and a mouthful of ugly sharp teeth. The smell was getting to me so I decide to end my driftwood hunt pronto. Even Whiskers was looking like she was going to puke. When I get home I hose the caked sand off the driftwood and set to cleaning and sorting each nature made work of art as if getting it ready for an art gallery. Once they are cleaned I will sand the pretty grained ones to bring out there beauty. The white bleached ones I'll leave alone.

Grandpa comes by and gives me the thumbs up.

"You got some good ones this time Lady Bug. But you shouldn't be drinking out of that dirty hose. Especially after using it to clean off gar slime."

"I'm just really thirsty, Grandpa. It's hotter than melted tar today." I think I get my artistic tendencies from Grandpa Frankie. Grandpa Frankie is a house painter and uses his left over paint to paint wonderful pictures of scenery on stretched out window shade canvas's. Jon E. and I are always beggin' Grandpa to paint us in his pictures. Grandpa has this giant sized fancy carved picture frame he bartered from a showboat in payment for painting fancy trim around their bar. He said it framed a mirror that got broke from a beer bottle being thrown in a fight over a dance hall girl. His dream is to one day paint a giant picture to fit the frame. As I said, He's a real artist so I can hardly wait for him to find time to paint his dream picture. Mom leans out the kitchen window to greet Grandpa.

"Come on in for some lemonade Pop. Have you finished your mail route yet?"

"Sure did Sweet-pea and I'd love some lemonade."

I hear them talking in the kitchen and hear Grandpa tell Mom a secret.

"My supervisor has been steaming open the letters again. That women is the nosiest, gossip I've ever meet. One of these days someone is going to notice their mail has been steamed open and their will be hell to pay."

I have never heard Grandpa use the h--- word before and I'm totally shocked. Mom glances out the window and notices my shocked reaction.

"Stop that eaves dropping and to stop fiddlin' with that smelly driftwood. I think you may need to burn that gunny sack it smells so bad. Hose it down and throw it over the back fence. Maybe if it sits out in the sun long enough the smell will evaporate. Then get your self inside and wash your hands with lye soap. One of these days you're going to get sick fooling with that dirty driftwood. I need you to take these snapdragons around to the neighbors and try selling them. You might take some of them down to Reatha's Florist Shop and see if she would like to buy some."

It has been a bumper crop this year. The snapdragons are gorgeous. You could get intoxicated just smelling them. I love pinching the flower heads and pretend they're jabbering. I hate trying to sell them. I'm tongue-tied shy around grownups and never know what to say. Usually I knock, thrust the flowers in the customers face and mumble "for sale". Then I wait red faced until they ask me how much or say no thanks. My mom, Velma Ann, sells snapdragon's in the summer and washes and irons other people's clothes to pay for piano lessons for both Jon E. and myself. To have piano lesson's was a dream she'd had as a child and she was determined we would get to live her dream. Even if chapped, wrinkled fingers, and an aching back were what she had to pay for it. Jon E. quit those lesson's and now plays "Rock and Roll" tunes by ear. He can really make a piano talk when pounding out tunes like "Rock With me Henry". Mrs. Warner was my first piano teacher but I was too scared to go to the Warner house by myself so Mom let me change teachers and I now go to a Mrs. Brody. She is so classy. I have no hope of being like her when I grow up but I sure wish I could. I prefer classical music. It stirs something in me. Sometimes it almost brings tears to my eyes, especially the "Moonlight Sonata." It makes me feel like my heart is crying when I play it. It's hard to explain but I love it. I can march up town to Rachmaninoff' or Beethoven as it plays in my head. One of the merchants commented to my mom about how straight and almost military I looked when walking uptown once. Little did he know it was because I was playing "March Militare" in my mind as I walked. My brother, Jon E., is a blooming genius. He got all the brains. It isn't fair. He likes to mean mouth me sometimes.

"Lou Ann, he says, "You must've been standing behind the lamp post when brains were handed out." So even at an early age I learned that life wasn't fair on so many levels. Back when he was in fourth grade Jon E. had tested out at a 170 IQ. He checked out and read the library's old encyclopedias as if they are his brain's cotton candy. His favorite sibling taunt is "Shit for Brains". It hurts because compared to him I know I really am just that…a shit for brains. Still it's grounds for chasing him around the outside of the house with a baseball bat. Jon E. learned to run real fast that way. Fast enough to get on the schools track team. So you could say I was his track coach.

11

A Season Of Pain

I feel kind of dizzy headed and don't eat much for supper. My head hurts. Nanny Jo, my next door neighbor, and I had played a few games of tennis on the back levee tennis court this morning and I'd gotten a little sick at my stomach from the heat. I figure I stayed out in the sun too long. Even my neck hurts. I hope it's not sunstroke. I feel listless and decide to go to bed early. I can't seem to find a comfortable spot and toss and turn restlessly. I'm sweating and feel like I'm going to puke. I beg Dad to keep the huge washing machine motor fan he rigged up and put in the attic to keep us cool on just a little while longer.

"We can't afford to keep it on all night honey but I'll wait until I go to bed before I turn it off."

I'm still awake when he gets in bed. The sound of the fan usually lulls me to sleep but somethings wrong tonight. I decide to just kick off the covers and keep cool that way, I wake up in the wee morning hours burning with fever and a headache. The pain... oh the pain in my right leg is so... so bad.

"Mama, Mama please come quick." I can't move Mama. It hurts Mama. It hurts bad!"

Mama comes running but nothing she does helps. She trys to move my leg and even touching me hurts. I scream bloody murder. It feels like pins and needles are in my leg. I try to be brave but it hurts so very much. She gets out the heating pad and puts it on my leg.

"Ben call Doc Hudson. His number is on the inside flap of the phone book. Tell him this is an emergence."

"Mama I feel like I'm going to throw up! Mom gets the waist basket just in time. I'm so weak I can't even roll over so she holds me up. My neck feels like a hot poker is in it. I can't turn my head without it hurting.

"Ben tell the Doc he needs to come immediately. No, wait, let me talk to him." I hear mom mumble something about Infantile Paralysis while talking on the phone. "She has all the symptoms Doc. Please hurry!" Mom gives a relieved sigh.

"Doc says he'll be here in thirty minutes. Mom puts a cool cloth over my eyes and I think about her words on the phone. And then it dawns on me. Oh no! That's what made Mr. Roosevelt a cripple. I start praying to God "Please God don't let it be that." Not polio! Please let me not be a cripple! I'll never complain again about not being on the boy's baseball team. I'll be a good girl and never again ask for the cowgirl outfit for Christmas. I won't even chase Jon E. with a baseball bat even if he does call me Shit for Brains." The room seems to spin when I open my eyes. I wonder if that means I have a fevor?

Doc Hudson arrives and gives me one of his 'I'll take care of you smiles.' He shakes down his thermometer and sticks it in my mouth.

"How are you feeling Lou Ann?" he asks.

Now how am I supposed to say anything with a thermometer in my mouth? He takes it out and wipes it down with alcohol. I notice he is wearing rubber gloves.

"She does have a slight fever." Velma Ann. Where do you hurt Lou Ann?"

"All over Doc." I whisper because I can't get enough breath to talk louder. "Pains mostly in my right leg and my neck. My leg feels like someone is stabbing me over and over. It hurts so much Doc. Can you make it stop?" I cry. "Please Doc make it stop!"

"Velma Ann the heating pad is a good idea but I want you to make it a moist heat. Put a warm wet towel under the heating pad and wrap it around her right leg. It will help soothe the pain."

"Can't you give her any medication to help with the pain Doc? She is really hurting. She is my tough girl and I've known her to bang her finger with a hammer and not even whimper. The fact that she is moaning and crying now means she has to be in extreme pain!"

"I'm sorry Velma Ann but if its what we fear I can't give her a narcotic. It increases the risk of a lung collapsing. We certainly don't want her to end up in an iron lung. I am going to take a mouth culture with this swab and send it to the lab. We will know for sure in a few days. There has been an outbreak. Her schoolmate Ruthie Barnes came down with it this weekend. It will just have to run its course if its what we fear.. and get out of her system. She'll have to be isolated. I'm putting a quarantine notice on your door. Polio is highly contagious. Jon E. is to steer clear of this room. You alone are to enter it.. I'll give you a supply of rubber gloves. And you wear them whenever you empty the chamber pot. You can't help Lou Ann if you get sick too. Its body fluids that are so contagious. Even your husband is not to enter the room."

I hear Papa protesting. "But that's my little girl in there Doc."

"I know Ben, but you can't take the risk of starting an epidemic around here. You can talk to her from the other room and make sure she has lots of fruit drinks. She needs those to get well but give them to Velma Ann to bring into the room. Now Velma Ann I want you to boil every cup, knife, fork and spoon she uses. In fact use the same one over and over just to be safe. And she is to use only a bed pan to relieve herself. Make sure when you empty it the toilet lid is not touched. Think like the sterile cleaning nurse you once went to school to learn to be. Am I clear Velma Ann?" Mama nods in mute agreement as if in shell shock.

"Let me give you a supply of rubber gloves." And don't get careless. Use them."

"Yes Doc, you know I will. How long will we be in quarantine?"

"At least 3 weeks. That means both Ben and Jon E. can't go to work or school that long. Have your grocery's delivered. "If we're lucky the pain will gradually recede. It may take 4 to 6 weeks for the infection to clear her system. But she may need as much as 6 months of bed rest before her leg muscles feel good enough to walk."

"But Doc her leg will atrophy if she doesn't move!

"You're correct Velma Ann. That's when you click into some kind of physical therapy. You must start it as soon as the virus clears her system. Move both her legs back and forth, up and down at least 30 minutes 3 times a day. It will be painful at first. But it must be done. Its going to be a long haul. But both you and Lou Ann are fighters so I know you can do it. The first month will be the hardest. After that you can start the leg work. I'll stop in every two weeks to check on the diseases progress the first two months."

"We can't afford you doing that Doc."

"I'll bill it to county health as stopping a polio epidemic. No need to pay me.

The first 6 weeks were pure hell for both me and my mom. I felt badly because mom looked so tired and worried. Even Jon E. looked worried. That scared me. After the disease ran its course I felt well enough to sit up and listen to someone read to me. Jon E. surprised me by volunteering to sit outside the bedroom door and be my reader. He read me the 'Swift Family Robinson' I'd started before I got ill. I so looked forward to hearing him read. I would lie with the cool cloth over my eyes and pretend I was in the book; fighting pirates, riding turtles, digging pits. It was so boring being unable to get out of bed. Mom made arrangements with the school so I could keep up with my classmates by doing all the lessons. I got the neatest hand made get well cards from my classmates. Bev Swinger even made me one with violets all over it. Jon E. brought all my assignments home and

I did all my lessons while in bed. The 30 minutes of leg movement was very painful at first, but Mom told me I would be cripple if I didn't work the leg. So I just bit my lip and clinched my fists and endured the pain. As the weeks turned into months and I got stronger it grew gradually less painful. I worked so hard that I was up and about in half the time first determined. Instead of 6 months in bed. I was only 3 months in bed. "How's my miracle child doing?" Doc would say when he checked in. At Christmas I was surprised by my best gift ever. I didn't know that Doc had told Dad that I needed a bike to strengthen my leg. So Dad found bike parts in the junkyard and made me a bike. He painted it blue. I thought it was the most beautiful thing I'd ever seen. Such a thing was never on my Santa list because I knew my parents couldn't afford such an expensive gift. Jon E. was the one that taught me to ride.

"Sit on the seat and pedal, he instructed. If you stop pedaling you'll crash."

I get on and he gives me a shove and I pedal. It was either pedal or crash. My brother didn't bother to tell me how to stop it. So I just coasted to a near stop and jumped off when I couldn't pedal any longer. I ran beside the bike happy as a lark. I now had wheels. I got really good at riding that bike. I named it Bella. I was no longer limited to just my home turf. I could ride all over town and I did. Jon E. even offered me a fraction of his paper route. I had Lowell street and the street over from it called 1st Street. As I think about the last year, I thank God for my recovery. I look at Whiskers, give her a hug and shout to the heavens. "Its a great big wonderful world! Life is such a wonder."

Lu Ann after surviving polio.

12

The Spelling Bee

My 5th grade home room teacher is the terror of the school. He is a Baptist minister on Sunday and rules his classroom as if Hell and Damnation was in all his students and he needed to stamp it out. Mr. Rockherd is his name and you'd better not forget it. He teaches cursive writing and spelling. His handwriting is like the wings of a song it is so graceful. He signs every official document the school needs signed. He's so old he looks to me as if he could've been a signer of the Declaration of Independence. Poor Jimmy Sender had even a worse hand writing than me. And he couldn't spell snot. That boy was jerked into a knot by Mr. Rockherd so many times he could have been a rosary bead.

"Mr. Rockherd" The principle needs you to sign some papers for him. Can you spare a minute?" says the secretary as she knocks on the classroom door.

"Certainly, I'll be right with you. Keep practicing your cursive writing class. Miss Swinger I'm leaving you in charge."

As soon as he leaves the room Jimmy jumps up and goes to the window to gaze out. He opens it and sits on the window ledge.

"Jimmy," I warn. You better sit down before you get in trouble."

"You better get back to your seat our I'll turn you in !" warns Bev the appointed class monitor. She is also one of the most popular girls in our class and a cheerleader.

"Geez don't let the power go to your Betsy Wetsy head." I mumble.

"Don't be such a fuss budget Bev. There's a great breeze coming in from the open window." argues Jimmy.

I almost go and join him because the room is indeed as hot as Hells back acres. But just then in walks Mr. Rockherd. Jimmy has his back to the door and doesn't see him step behind him.

"Ahem," goes Mr. Rockherd and before Jimmy can turn around he picks him up by the seat of his pants and tosses him out the window. Now this is in a second story room so we all assume he has just killed Jimmy. We hear a loud "thunk" and I rush over to see if Jimmy is still alive. Jimmy is sitting on the roof of the utilities shed which is just below the window rubbing his head. No one and I mean no one ever got out of their seat again in Mr. Rockherd's class. My favorite game in Mr Rockherd's class was the dictionary game. He would shout out a word and whoever found it the fastest was the winner. I usually won. I'm a competitor to the nth degree. Always have been and always will be. But the fact that I won and always passed my spelling test led Mr. Rockherd into a false assumption. I really am not a good speller. So what happens. He puts me in as a contestant in a Spelling Bee that is going to be broadcast over the radio.

"Mama I don't want to be in the Spelling Bee. Can't you tell him I'm sick or something?"

"I will not lie for you Lou Ann. You will just have to give it your best shot."

"That's an idea! Maybe brother could shoot me with his Red Rider BB gun?"

"Don't be a silly goose. I'm not letting Jon E. shoot you." laughs Mom. So off I go to the Spelling Bee. We were tied and our opponents were up. They were given the word that means the act of choosing.

"C-h-i-o-c-e" spells the other team member.

"Wrong!" the judges state. It's my turn. I am shaking in my boots because I know its the old {oi} rule. I step up to the microphone in a daze and spell it "C-h-i-o-c-e". Oh my God! As soon as it came out of my mouth I knew I'd goofed. I'd just had the old frozen from fear brain syndrome You could hear the gasp from my fellow classmates fill the sound booth. So the game went on and the other team won. End of story and end of fooling Mr. Rockherd into thinking I really could spell.

It's not fair! I play ball as good as the boys!

13

Call To Vote

Two years have passed and I'm in the 6th grade now. I've graduated to the upstairs now and considered a young lady. Ha Ha not! Sitting on the front steps folding the Evening Citizen I confide to my dog Whiskers.

"I wish I were a boy."

Whiskers pants her understanding, and comes over to give me a comforting lick.

"Boys get to do all the fun things in the world like own a paper route."

"Woof, Woof," goes Whiskers.

Encouraged by the understanding bark I grumble on.

"When they grow up they get to be explores, inventors, and star athletes. All kinds of great things. They also get to play baseball on the school team."

All this grumbling is because my grade school coach had just petitioned the school board to get me on his baseball team. I was that good. I could out hit the boys and play a mean shortstop. But I had just found out the school board out voted my Dad and the coach and flat out refused the petition. When he told me their reason I just exploded.

"Heaven forbid if I got hit in the boobs with a line drive. What a piece of drivel for an excuse that is."

"I'm sorry Lou Ann. I sure could have used you." laments Coach Kellis.

"That just isn't fair!" I scream with tears in my eyes.

Just isn't fair is beginning to be my mantra. My good friend, Gi Gi, who is the grade school principles daughter, comes over to sit on the porch and help me fold papers. There's a trick to folding it star shaped so it could be tossed from the sidewalk right up to a customer's front door. She lived just up the street and was a year older than me. Just like Mom and Dad I was Mutt to her Jeff. You know like the cartoon characters where one was short, that would be me, and one was tall, that would be Gi Gi. Her real name is Georgia.

"Did you hear that your Dad and mine are going to call a vote for consolidating the black and white schools tonight?" she asked. "I'm really scared. Dad got a lot of scary phone call threats today."

"I'm scared too." I heard mom crying and begging Dad not to do it. But Dad said he was going to call the vote come hell or high water. Jon E. and his best friend Johnny are going to climb up to the storage shed roof and watch. Could you sit on the porch and wait until I get back from delivering papers? I want to ask a favor of you when I get back."

"Sure Lou Ann. Mom's inside visiting with your mom anyway."

I hurry through my short deliveries and sit down beside Gi Gi. "See this here baseball bat," I say as I wave it bravely in the air. "I'm going to go to stand in front of the school house doors and bash anyone that threatens my Dad. Nobody's going to shoot my Daddy while I'm around! Would you pretend you're talking to me so that mom won't know I've left the porch?"

"Oh Lou Ann! Don't do that! That's too dangerous." begs Gi Gi as she grabs my arm.

About that time I see Grant Valley drive up and park in front of the grade school in his police car. He gets out and just stands in front of the school looking like a Mack truck or maybe a big black brick wall. Hog Plover comes with a shotgun in the crook of his arm and tries to pass. Grant blocks his way and just talks to him quietly. Then he takes his gun and lets him enter the school unarmed. Gi Gi and I look at each other and grab hands in relief.

"Guess I don't need go protect anyone with my baseball bat." The fear and tension in the air is palpable. Mom and Gi Gi's mom come from inside the house and sit in the front porch swing as night comes and street lights go on. We hear Hog Plover's voice as he jerks a window open on the grade school's second floor study hall.

"It's hotter than hell in here. Don't this here school got no fans?" he grumbles.

We hear a gavel pounded and Principal Lee call the meeting to order. Bits of conversation can be heard from the window. It's all mundane things. They drone on and on about book fees, equipment needed, teacher tenure then all the sudden we hear screaming and cussing coming from the open school window. Gi Gi and I get a real education in cussing that night. It was @##$ this and @#$ that. Gi Gi and I just look at each other and put our hands over our mouths. The cicadas had started their droning. Their little legs drummed on their tiny bellies until the night air vibrated their song. They were almost loud enough to drown out the blaring hate that was broadcast from the school window. We peer at the shadows of Jon E. and Johnny listening to the proceedings on the shed roof. My brother's best friend, Johnny is Willa Mae's brother. Willa Mae and I sometimes play hopscotch together. She's always asking me to play dolls, but I'm not into that kind of sissy stuff. Suddenly there is a great cheer and the boys scuttle down the storage shed's drainpipe and jump to the playground. As they come running over we all shout.

"What happened?"

Brother was so angry he was trembling.

Then between gritted teeth he said, "Well they tried. You got to give our Dads that. It was voted against hands down. But, by golly, the black schools are getting brand new school books from now on. Not the page torn, cover less, moldy, hand me downs that's been forced on them before. Dad said he would call the State School Board Commission on them if they didn't straighten up and fly right. It was a small victory but it was something."

Johnny nods his head in agreement. Johnny is a silent boy. I think about how I've never heard that boy talk out loud. He just whispers as if afraid to be heard. The boys go to the backyard to play a little catch. Gi Gi and I whisper together so the grownups can't hear us.

"I've got the perfect name for Johnny. It should be Ghost. Don't you think that's the perfect name for him? I kind of like him but don't you dare tell anyone that. Cross your heart and hope to die."

I chatter on to Gi Gi like a magpie. "Don't you think he's cute? He is as thin as a bean pole. But he's wiry strong he is. With five mouths to feed in his family grub just isn't plentiful. According to Willa Mae, Johnny's sister, it's beans everyday; white beans, pole bean, pinto beans, baked beans, red beans or Lima beans. Some kind of beans everyday. I'd sure starve to death if I were in that family because I hate beans. I barely tolerate pork and beans but lima beans just gag me."

"They are yucky!" agrees Gi Gi. "I hate Lima beans too."

"Mom let me invite Willa Mae to supper one time and she had never had a yeast roll before. Can you imagine that?"

Gi Gi just shakes her head in disbelief. I didn't tell Gi Gi because it would be hurtful gossip but Mom told me to always refuse dinner offers from Willa Mae because it would be like taking food out of her family's mouth. I caught Johnny stealing a drink out of a bottle of milk that had been delivered to his neighbor's back porch one time. I guess they don't get milk at their house either. No wonder he is so frail looking. Mom doesn't know it but I'm too scared of their father to ever sit down at a table with him. He is big, strong and growly. I saw him whip Johnny with a belt once so hard it scared the bejeebers out of me. Sometimes I have nightmares about him coming after me with an ax. My wild imagination gets me in trouble a lot. They live just down the street from us and have a pig sty in their backyard. I guess they're planning on having pork and beans forever.

I then start telling Gi Gi about the little baby chicks Grandma Shears is breedin' in her kitchen.

"They are so cute Gi Gi." She keeps them in her kitchen so they can incubate near her Warm Morning stove." I explain. "You must keep them very warm are they might die. She lets me play with them when I go over. I'm real careful."

I think about how we sure will have some great fried chicken when her 'peepers' grow up. Then it dawns on me. I'm a cannibal! The thought doesn't stop me from craving fried chicken though.

"Did you know chickens are as dumb as rocks?" I ask Gi Gi.

"Really?, Why do you say that?"

"Brother is always hypnotizing them by drawing a line in the dirt with a stick and sticking their beaks on the line. They won't move come hell or high water. It is so funny to watch. Then when he pulls their becks off the line they stagger around like they're drunk. Grandma gets yelling mad at Jon E. for doing that. Said it makes them so goofy they forget to lay eggs. I watched Grandpa wring a chicken's neck once for Mama. It walked around without a head for almost 2 minutes."

"Yuck. That's gross, Lou Ann."

"I'll tell you something that's grosser. That's when Mama sticks them in boiling water to loosen the feathers for plucking. There is nothing that stinks more than wet scalded chicken feathers. Just thinking about it makes me gag."

As I talk to Gi Gi about these things I glance up at Mrs. Lee. She just looks down at me, shakes her head and smiles. Its like she's saying, 'There goes Lou Ann telling whoopers again." But its true! chickens are dumber than rocks.

Mrs. Lee has the sweetest smile when she isn't worried. In fact Mrs. Lee could tame a rabid wild dog with her smile. Not that there are any rabid wild dogs around. Except for maybe the human kind like Hog Plover.

"Anyone want a cool glass of lemonade and cookies? asks mom.

"Thanks, Velma Ann" says, Irma May. I sure could use something to cool me down. We all yell a hardy yes and retire to the kitchen for lemonade and cookies as we await our two knights in shiny amour's return. When Dad and Mr. Lee, who also happens to be my grade school principal, enter the kitchen we all give them a loud cheer. WE are all so very proud of them for what they had attempted. You could see the disappointment on their faces but that cheer perked them up a little. My principal shook my Dad's hand as they left and said, "Thank you for supporting me Ben. I'll never forget it."

Dad shook hands with Principal Lee and said, "I'm proud to be your friend. It was just the right thing to do. Think nothing about it. And Henry, mark my word. Consolidation will happen someday. Maybe not in our lifetimes, but some day."

A sad Principal Lee after the No vote for consolidation.

14

Collection Days

As you may remember, my bike's name is Bella. She's named after one of my favorite classical piano composers, Bella Bartok. I can pedal her so fast you'd think I was flying. I love my bike. It's my freedom rider. I collect for my brother's paper route every Saturday on Bella. I go up town and down town, near and far collecting the hard earned pennies of my customers. I even collect from taverns. One tavern owner is soft spoken like my Dad.

"Little lady," he says, "Just wait outside the door a second and I'll get your money."

The message to me was clear. 'Little ladies don't go into a tavern. The tavern clientele seem to reflect the persona of their owners. Thus, I found out there were such things as mean drunks and mellow drunks. My brother, Jon E. collects from the mean drunk taverns and the black taverns. He can jolly up most people and I was glad to not have to do any jollying. On the deadbeats we would team up. I would knock on the front door and when they would run out the back door he would be waiting there. I collect from the old and the young, the sighted and the blind, from the poor and the rich, from the black and the white. Your learn a lot about people from collecting. It's strange. The sweet deaf and dumb lady that lives all alone in the big house across the highway seems to see beyond others seeing. I don't know why they called her dumb. She's as sharp as a tack! I'm going to have to ask my Mama about that. I knock on her door and she "hears" me and she can't hear. How does she do that? It's a mystery. I know she couldn't hear my kick stand going down. But she always had a cookie and a smile waiting for me when she opened the door. How does she "hear" my knock? It's a mystery. She always motions me in, gives me a cookie, and asks about the news of the neighborhood. She talks to me by notepad and pencil. She is a speed writer. Her words seem to race right across the pad. She must read lips to because she always understands what I say. I suspect she is just lonely and wants company. Just because she's different the kids treat her like she's a witch or something scary. The adults aren't much better. They laugh at her behind her back and avoid her. It hurts me when I hear the neighbor kids taunt her.

As I leave the house I hear a boy shouting at Mrs. Darling.

"Dummy, Dummy you're so crummy." Thank goodness she can't hear him. But I do and that's just down right mean. I turn and spot Tommy Jones being the culprit.

"You say that again Tommy Jones and I'll chase you down with my bike and run right over your mealy- mouthed sorry ass."

I jump on Bella and zoom arrow fast toward him. He jumps over his fence so I miss him by just inches. I did whack him with a stick though while whizzing by. It was another thing I had to add to my list of what just wasn't fair. A lady as nice as Mrs. Darling should have lots of friends not mean kids taunting her. I always stay as long as I dare visiting with Mrs. Darling but collection day is a really busy day for me.

The poor people with many children seem strangely rich and happy. The older siblings are always looking after the younger ones. Last Saturday

I saw 5 year old Sherry Young changing the diaper of her baby brother, Ben and then picking up her new born sister Jen and giving her a bottle. Meanwhile their mom cooks pork and beans on the coal stove. She seems to be always washing out soaked diapers. They always invite me inside to warm up on a cold day and offer up a warm cup of hot chocolate. It smelled of dirty diapers, cooking beans, hot chocolate and love to me. Some of the so called rich are niggerdly with the warmth of their homes or the warmth of their hearts. For instance, I'm never invited in, even on the coldest of days to warm up my frozen hands at the banker's house. I often talk to myself as I ride my bike on winter collection days bundled up like an Eskimo in Alaska. People probably think I'm crazy. But it helps keep my mind off the cold.

"Mr. Tight in the Breeches," that's what I call the banker, "you're just like Charles Dicken's Scrooge. A real bah humbug sort of guy. Don't you know money can't buy happiness."

The way everyone scrambles for it would make you think it does. But it really doesn't. Sure makes you wonder what does. As I said before. I'm good at wondering. Delivering papers is just like delivering mail. "Come wind, come rain, come snow, come sleet and come the coldest day of the year the paper must be delivered. Well, today is Sunday and the temperature has dropped to -16 degrees Fahrenheit. You can't fold the Sunday paper into stars. It's much too thick. The Sunday paper has the front page news, a lifestyle section, local news, sports, an advertisement section, obits and funny papers. For once Mom lets us bring the delivered stack of papers into the front room so we can fold and tuck the larger newspapers into compact small rectangles. As I put my devied up folded papers into my canvas delivery sack Mom calls out from the kitchen.

"Go slip on the ski pants your Aunt Ruby Ann sent you from California for Christmas Lou Ann."

Aunt Ruby Ann was now living with Grandma's sister in California and working as a secretary for an Import and Export Company. It seems the lawyer's wife had caught them in a 'compromising position" (what ever that means) and she got fired. I think she's better off now if you want my opinion. I do as suggested because the ski pants just slip over my jeans and are extra warm.

"Jon E. go get the hand warmers your Grandpa got you guys for Christmas. I believe they're in the tool box. I'll get them started for you. And both of you need to put on an extra pair of socks with your boots."

Mom comes into the front room wiping her hands on her dish towel. She looks at Dad and nods.

"Son, it's too dangerous for you to be out delivering so long in this cold. I'm going to take you around in the car."

I've never seen such a relieved and surprised look on Jon E.'s face.

"Thank you Dad. I really appreciate that!"

"Do you want to wait until we're finished so that I can take you around Pumpkin?"

"No Dad. I only have two blocks to deliver. I can take the sled and get it done quicker and faster that way." By the time I finished my route and got home my hands were starting to feel like icycles. My legs were fairly warm but my feet felt like they were a solid block of ice.

"Mama, I can't feel my feet," I cried. Mom had me take off my ski pants and boots and double layer of socks and gently rubbed my feet. Then she put my feet in a pot of cool water. It felt hot but it wasn't. Then she gradually heated it up. When my feet first started thawing out I wanted to scream bloody murder. But I didn't. Tough Tomboys don't scream. They may moan but they don't scream.

15

Muscles versus Mussels

Winter turns to spring and Brother Jon E. and his buddies decide to ride their bikes to Mudsville by going over the back levee road rather than riding down the highway. It's only three miles away as the crow fly's. But that road is much more crooked than a flying crow. The guys all gather at our house with their sack lunches and water canteens pretending they're explorers. That's because we live just a few blocks from the back levee. They make a sorry lot of explorers if you ask me.

"Its going to be a great. We can check out the back lot of the National Cemetery on the way to see if they have dug any new graves lately. We'll need to be careful. That grave keeper is one mean dude. I heard he whips that mutt of his so much that its as mean as a badger." informs my brother.

"Can I go to? Pretty please with sugar on top. I'm a real strong rider." I beg.

Skeeter mocks me and says, "Girls can't ride that far, only boys. Just because your a tomboy doesn't make you as strong as a boy."

Skeeter is a skinny kid that I could beat arm wrestling with my eyes closed.

So I stick my tongue out at him and yell, "I'm as strong as you twerp and you know it."

Mom hushes me and much to my surprise says, "Girls your age shouldn't be tagging along with boys. So, no, you may not go Lou Ann and that's that."

"What the devil is being a girl got to do with it? I say in shock.

But Jon E. just says," get lost brat. Go play with your dolls."

Jon E. knows I don't play with dolls. Never have and never will. Mom gets me a beautiful doll every Christmas. I just smile, thank her, dress and undress it a few times and put it in my closet for the rest of the year. I even got a boy doll once. It was my favorite but it still went into the closet. My Aunt Ruby Ann got me a bride doll last Christmas with real hair. My mom got so mad at me for cutting its hair short I almost got a spanking. But a doll with long hair is a sissy doll and who wants a sissy doll.

"Why don't you go to the front levee and collect some prize mussels. I'll get you a gunny sack you can fill up. Your collection could use some new, interesting specimens. The storm two nights ago should have washed a lot of shells up on the banks. I'll fill up a canteen for you with some Kool Aid. What kind would you like?"

"Do you have any strawberry Kool Aid?"

"Sure do. I'll go make you a batch. Would you like a peanut butter sandwich too."

"That would be great! Thank you Mom. Could you put a dab of honey in it?" I ask surprised at how nice she was treating me.

The guys take off and I take my gunny sack and Dad's old lunch pail full of the treats Mom has made for me. As I watch then leave I'm envious.

I mumble to myself, "Guys get to do all the interesting things. It just isn't fair." I ride up town and over to the front levee. There are cutout steps in the front levee. I walk my bike up the steps and park my bike at the top of the levee. I look down at the mighty Ohio river and see a tug boat named Nanny

Jo pushing coal up the river. Nanny Jo is the warehouse owner's daughter. "How cool is that having a tug boat named after you," I ponder with envy. Its such a wide river I really can't see well to the other shore. I do see the sandbar in the middle, however. I hear that some boys and girls go skinny dipping at night and swim to that sandbar. You won't catch me doing such a stupid thing! I wonder how much bigger an ocean can possibly be. I look down to the river bank below me and see that Mom is right. The bank is absolutely littered with shells. I excitedly scramble down the rocky levee. I've taken along my "Mollusk Collector's Book of Identification" hoping to find a rare river mussel for my collection. There are lots of finger nail or peg clams. There is a mix of dull brown and rust shells of this petite clam. I scoop up a handful to look through for perfect unchipped examples. I have a lot of those already. I spot a thin, finger long, dull moss green shell and look it up in my book. "Wow" I think I've got me a Duck mussel." I find one that is rust colored and one that is brown and stick them both in my gunny sack. I wander around and down by my left foot I spot a bivalve that is a golden brown and has a bump like a nose. I clean off the sand and pull it apart. The insides are a beautiful iridescent pearly color. I wash the meat out in the river water and drop it in my sack carefully. "Don't want to break that beauty", I mutter to myself. I spot another one the same shape but black on the outside. Sure enough its the same kind and the book says there are black ones too. "Hot diggity", I say as I pump my arm in a truck driver horn plea. Wiping my hands on my jeans I scan the pictures in my guide book and I find I have found a Sheepnose mussel. This is a lot more fun than riding a bike down a dusty road and eating some ones dirt I tell myself. I then spot an ugly green/brown long shell and almost throw it away its so ugly but decide to check it out in my guide book first. I'm surprised to find it's a rare clam called a Rabbitsfoot mussel. There goes Mommy's saying again about how you can't tell the book by its cover. I stroll along lazy like and I find a bunch of yellow sandshells. They aren't so rare but they are pretty. I spot a pretty dark ebony shell.

"Still haven't found an elkstoe, a monkeyface, or a gray billyput." I mumble "I don't think I'm ever going to find a fat musket or pistelgrip mussel but I'm gettin' hungry." So I sit down and eat my prepared lunch. The sun is at noon high and its getting hot and stinky on the levee. I decided to save searching for those treasures for another day and climb back up to my bike careful not to twist my ankle on the uneven ground. I walk my bike down the cutout steps and ride home. Droppin' my sack in the backyard I hurriedly sort out my find. A surprise thought came to me. "I bet I had a better time than those dumb old boys."

The smell of dead gar and wet muddy sand clings to the mussels. So I unwind the water hose and attach it to the backyard facet. I carefully spread my findings on the backyard walkway. After hosing them down thoroughly I let the sun dry them off and go inside to practice my piano. Its been a fun day I decide. I go out after practice and pack up my collection in my shoe boxes making sure to label each new find. Jon E comes dragging in right before supper braying like a billy goat and smelling like one.

"Take off your shoe's son, and leave them outside. I think you've stepped in a cow paddy. What happened? "asks Mom.

"Skeeter's chain broke just a mile past the levee. He was nothing but a whining wimp the whole trip. I told him to put a sock in it."

"Pay back time, I think maliciously.

"Then Jimmy Sender's bike had a flat just as we reached the graveyard and the graveyard dog almost got us before we got away. Johnny got his pant leg ripped by the dog before the owner cursed us out and pulled off the dog.. His Dad is going to kill him for that. Those were brand new breeches."

Jon E. puts a wet washcloth on his head and announces, "I think I'm having a heat stroke."

"Oh yes. Pay back time for sure. My day has been so much better," I think suppressing a smirk. Then with a knowing Cheshire Cat smile I give Jon E. a well deserved cold shoulder for the rest of the evening. Just out of principle you see.

"Telling me to go play with my dolls." Get real twerp!" I mumble to myself.

BODACIOUS @7/12/2000

by Nancy Louise Weiser
(from Passion's Fire poetry book)

I was bodacious, oh yes,
The pain of genetic whim.
"Here comes Robin Redbreast,?
Sneered boys with monkey limbs.

They punched each others shoulders,
Then drooled like dirty old men
At girls that walked the gauntlet
With blushes and embarrassed grins......

16

Bodacious

The years pass uneventfully then all the sudden I find myself in the sixth grade. It seems like over night that my buds grew. They grew into melons. Round fully packed melons! I am so, so, so embarrassed. Even the older girls don't have melons yet. Its not fair! Boys are looking straight at my chest! I don't want a chest! Cheerleaders like having guys stare at their chest. I'm a tomboy not a cheerleader! At my last birthday party I had to chase down and tackle the boy who was supposed to kiss me after winning the spin in "spin the bottle". I've had to pretend to like shy, blond skinny-legged Paulie since the first grade so the rest of the girls would get off of my case. Why one was expected to have a boyfriend I don't know. Boys are like spider monkeys. All arms and legs and they smell like old gym socks. And now they are X-raying my chest. Mom can't figure out why I refuse to wear sweaters now. She never had breast so doesn't understand why I want to hide in too big sweat shirts. Now she wants to take me to Karo to a department store and get me fitted for a bra. I may just die. Actually,

I want to just lie down and die. We get on the bus and the smell of the exhaust fumes almost makes me want to barf. It's a hot summer day. A kind of day only a lizard can love. I sit beside mom dressed in a starched white shirt and my skirt. It had little flowers all over it. Mom had gotten the material from a flour sack. My black and white saddle oxfords are well polished and looking spiffy. I even have on fancy white cotton socks that Grandma had trimmed with her doily making needles. Mom forced me to take off my blue jeans and put on a skirt. I feel strange all dressed up like I'm going to church just to ride on the bus. I pout as we ride in total silence. It should be a big event for me go all alone with my Mom shopping. Riding the bus all the way to the big city of Karo is not an everyday occurance. I hardly ever get store bought clothes. Mom is a great seamstress and makes most of our clothes. She even made me a linen coat for Easter once that was pretty and white. I've never been shopping except pretend shopping from the Sears & Robuck Catalogue. That's our dream book. Every Christmas I'd pick out a picture of the baby brother or sister I waned but never got from that catalogue. Every year I have also asked for a cowgirl outfit just like Dale Rodgers that's in the catalogue. You know, the one with a cowgirl hat, jeans, long sleeved cowgirl shirt with a fringed vest and cowgirl boots just like Dale Rodgers. She is no wimp. She can ride a horse. My mind races around thinking of everything except the fact that someone is going to see and measure my breast. Will it be a man or a young woman or an old lady that does the breast touching and measuring? Mom points out Magnolia Mansion as we pass it. The Magnolia trees are in beautiful bloom. The glossy blossums are as big as a saucer. We pass the Public Library on Abraham Lincoln Ave. I am amazed by the size of it. I can't image how many wonderful books they must have in that library. We get off the bus in downtown Karo and I see the Jewel Theater in all its glory. The whole family went to see "Gone With The Wind" in that movie theater last year. Mom pulls me into a store with a big display of fancy dresses in the window. My lip begins to tremble. "Mama do I really need to get a bra? I could just tape them down."

"No Lou Ann, that is not an option. You're getting to be a young lady, at least physically if not emotionally and you don't want your breast flopping around."

"My God! Do my breast flop now? Is that what the boys are staring at."

"Don't curse Lou Ann. You straighten up and fly right before I whip your behind right in front of God and Country!"

I am mortified at the thought of flopping breast along with being whipped in public and aburptly stop my protesting seeing that my whining isn't working. Mom seeks out a nice elderly women clerk and in what seems like a mega phone voice says,

"Do you have any training bras"

"Not so loud Mama!" I say my face turning a deep purple.

"Yes we do, but she will need to be measured first."

The women takes me into a thick curtain covered dressing room and asks me to take off my shirt. Noticing my embrassement and feeling sorry for me she says,

"Do you want your mother to come in and be with you."

"No mam," I reply.. Wanting to prove how mature and brave I was. She then measures how round each breast is and then how wide a chest I have. Strangely she didn't make me feel embarrassed. Just like it was a normal thing to do. She told Mom I didn't need a "training" bra. That I'm a normal 24 B. And that a "training" bra would be too small. To my surprise Mom bought me not one but two bras. As a special treat Mom took me to a cowboy matinee at the Jewel Theater. They had seats that felt like velvet and it was air conditioned inside. We saw a movie that starred my favorite singing cowboy Roy Rodgers and the Sons of the Pioneers. The song "Happy Trails My Friends" seemed to linger in my mind. I realized all my stupid fretting had been for nothing. I'd had a wonderful day. Although wearing a bra still feels funny. But at least I won't be flopping and I can go back to wearing some of my nice sweaters. As we take the bus back home and go under the levee underpass I think about how Karo is a city inside two levees. A levee on its backside for the Ohio River and a levee on its front side for the Mississippi River. Where they meet at the bridge to Kentucky you can see the blue waters meeting the muddy brown. When it mixes it looks like Karo syrup. I wonder if that's why people call it Karo? That's what I do best is wonder. In my minds eye I see Karo citizens really checking the river stages every night. I know I would if I were inside such a fish bowl.

Christmas season approaches and I no longer ask for a cowgirl outfit or a baby sister. In fact the glitter seems to have gone out of the season for me. The town is all astir about getting a life-sized manger scene. The City Council had ordered Three Kings, a Baby Jesus in a Crib and Mary and Joseph. Many citizens stand around watching as they start setting it up between the cracked Liberty Bell monument and the gazebo library on Main Street. "Papa where is the third king?" I ask. I only see two."

"You've got me Pumpkin." That is weird. I'll ask around." Papa goes over to the major and asks him the "Twenty-four dollar "question. When Papa comes back he looks angry and like he is going to burst out laughing at the same time. He gathers the whole family around and trying to keep a straight face he whispers. "They've got him locked up in a jail cell."

"Your talking crazy Ben," declares Mom.

"I'm not kidding. Our ignorant mayor didn't know one of the Wisemen would be black. He ordered it to be hidden in a jail cell at the county jail."

"But papa, our Sunday School Teacher, Mrs. Winkle, told us that Balthasar was from Arabia, Melchior was from Persia and Gasper was from India. That means ALL of the Wisemen were BLACK!"

"I know that. You know that. Your teacher knows that. But evidently our mayor didn't know that. I'll go try to post bond for Balthasar." Evidently he was painted blacker than the rest of them. (a repressed laugh breaks out and is quickly stiffed.) "But until then it's zip your lips everyone. That's an order! The city council paid for theses statues so the mayor doesn't have a right to ban Balthasar. And for heavens' sake. Please don't tell anyone where the Wiseman is stashed. We'll be the laughing stock of the whole county if the newspapers get hold of this story."

So I can proudly state it was because of Papa's jail breaking skills that all Three Wise-men stood guard over the manger scene during the Christmas of 1953.

17

Dear Old Golden Rule Days

As I go into high school I go through many changes to my tomboy lifestyle.

"Lou Ann, according to this high school requirement list you can no longer wear jeans to school. You must wear sweaters or blouses and skirts or even a dress," informs Mom.

"Why not? I like to wear jeans. They look perfectly fine to me. They are neat and clean." I say in protest.

"Rule are rules. Don't shoot the message bearer. It's not lady like according to the school letter. It goes under the heading of young ladies high school dress code." quotes Mom.

"I'm not a lady. I'm a tomboy." I protest. I bet boys get to wear jeans."

"Of course they do. But they can't wear muscle shirts or tank tops.

"Can I at least still wear my black and white saddle oxfords?"

"I promise to keep them polished."

Many of the girls are wearing those fancy penny loafers now but not me. Some boys even wear them and put a dime instead of a penny in the top flap.

"According to the school rules that is fine. Just no toeless sandels it says." informs Mom.

I look at my class schedule and see I have gym on Tuesdays. I look forward to gym until I find out what we're forced to wear.

"This here thing is the gosh darn uglyest gym suit I've ever seen!" I whisper loudly in my friend's ear. Bev looks like she's gonna cry because of having to wear it. Bev is a petite, prim, brunette and never ever has a shirt tail pulled out or a hair out of place unlike myself. It was a one piece blue cotton shirt attached to a blue bloomer.

"They smell gross like boys jock straps." she complains as she holds her nose.

I think, "How does she know what a jock strap smells like?" Then I remember her brother is on the basketball team. Boys get to wear basketball shorts and a sleeveless tank tops in gym. It just isn't fair. Other first time experiences tarnish my tomboy image big time. I try out for chorus piano accompanist with the encouragement of my neighbor Nanny Jo Krane, and much to my surprise I make it. Her brother could play rings around me but he was out of school now. I'm informed I must wear a formal gown to accompany for the musical "Gypsy Fortune Teller." "You'll need to wear hose and heels too," informs Mom. "You must shave your legs and wear a garter belt too.

"But Mom I'm just playing the piano not going to a stupid prom." I protest. "How do you shave your legs?"

"You can use one of your Dad's razors and his shaving cream. Just be careful and don't press too hard." Needless to say I came out of the shaving experience with many nicks and cuts and legs spotted with bits of toilet paper. Sitting on the piano bench I felt like I was topless because my shoulders were bare. I wasn't myself. My tomboy self was all wrapped up in a different package. Walking with heels felt like I was walking on strapped on tomato juice cans which I had done for fun in grade school. The whole time I was playing I felt weird. Just plain weird. Almost like I was a young lady. Am I changing? I do wonder. And as you know, that's what I do best.

18

Kissing Games

My first kissing game was at my 13th birthday party which was three years ago.

"Lou Lou is a teenager," chanted the boys and girls.

I felt almost like a girl all dressed up in a party dress that day. It was a pale pink dress with loop trim at the bodice and sleeves. Now I was never a girl that liked pink. But this was my teen party so it was acceptable.

"Mom, can I have boys and girls at my party," I'd begged.

"Sure but no more than 12 people. The house isn't big enough to hold more."

I'll invite 6 boys and 6 girls then." I invite KP for my brother. She's my friend too but brother begs me to invite her. I think he has a crush on her. She is a petite girl that is a cheerleader. He got to know her from his paper route. He said she wore this almost flimsy see through blouse when he would come to collect from her parents. No wonder he wanted me to invite her.

"You'll own me I warn brother," as I add her name to my list.

It was going to be a fun day with a homemade birthday cake and store bought ice cream.

"Time to play Pin the Tail on the Donkey." announces Mom. I got so spun around that I pinned the Tail on the sofa. I got a big laugh out of that. Gi Gi won that game. I don't think she cheated. The blindfold was pretty thick. She just has a real good sense of direction. I don't have any sense of direction. Brother says I was standing behind a fence post when directions were handed out. He's said that about my brains too.

"Lets play Spin the Bottle." suggests KP. Now the rules to Spin the Bottle were that the boy closest to the stopped pointing bottle had to kiss the girl doing the spinning and vise-versa. Well, it came my turn and the spin stops on my old school buddy, Lawrence Hooper. Lawrence is too much of a mouthful of a name so everyone calls him Curley instead.

"Curley's got to kiss Lou Ann" chant the party goers. Curley lived in a house with an Indian mound in his front yard. He was the son of a sweet lady that ran a beauty salon that I sometimes went to to get "gussied up" as my granny called it. I would empty all the waste baskets out on the floor to tease him knowing that he earned his allowance money by sweeping up the shop. Lawrence had beautiful, black, naturally curly hair. It was so pretty one wanted to run there fingers through his hair. I had to get perms to look as good as he did. Well to make a long story short at the birthday party Curley pips up and says,

"Oh no I'm not." You trashed the shop yesterday. I know it was you." said Curley laughing as he ran away to escape kissing me.

"Come back here you coward, I yell, laughing over the chasing fun. I chased him down and tackled him. I got him in a head lock and ended up kissing the top of his head. So my very first boy kiss was because I could tackle well.

A few years later my other practice kissing was the result of traveling on the school bus to basketball games. The boy I had declared my so called love interest in the First grade now played basketball. It was hands off for the other girls for they knew they would get a bloody nose. I would trap poor Paulie in the bus seat by sitting by him. He had the cutest legs in his basketball outfit. But he was so shy. I think I bruised his poor unresponsive lips trying to pretend great passion on those trips. It was like kissing a fence post. There was no "tongue" or what the other girls called "French kissing. The thought of sticking my tongue in his mouth just gagged me.

Then there were the dance parties that Bev held at her house on weekends when her mom was at work. She would pull up the rugs and bring out her collection of 45s. Bev was a cheerleader and had lots of friends. She could really dance too. She looked as good as a movie star dancing. Brother Jon E. always came to the parties with his older classmates. Gi Gi and I were kind of like the wallflowers at the party but we always went anyway. We were in charge of the record player.

"Lets play 'You've Lost That Lovin' Feelin' by the Righteous Brothers suggests Gi Gi. Then I would careful put the needle down. Bev would kill me if I scratched any of her treasured records. As usual neither of us got asked to dance.

"Oh look! Here's 'Pretty Woman' by Roy Orbenson. I've heard he's really good. Its a little livelier so it kind of perks up the party.

"Put on something romantic," prods Bev. I know she is wanting to dance close with the youngest Hopper boy. He is the cutest boy in our class. Never a hair is out of place on that boy's head.

"How about 'My Special Angel' by the Vogues," I suggest. "Perfect" she quips and boldly asks him to dance. Gi Gi and I just look through the 45 records. What a collection she has. There's "Hey There Lonely Girl by Eddie Holman, 'I Only Have Eyes For You by Frank Sinatra and 'The Great Pretender' by The Platters. I decide to put Old Blue Eye's song on. I see Bev whisper in Harry's ear and he comes over to ask me to dance. I am red faced and stumbling through the whole dance but at least I got to dance. When the dance ends I thank Harry and he looks at me like I'm weird. Was he supposed to be the one thanking me? I didn't have a clue. I go back and sit with Gi Gi. We look through another group of records.

"How about 'Love Me Tender' by Elvis Presley or 'April Love' by Pat Boone", I suggest.

"Naw, I want to hear the new Platters Song, 'Only You and You Alone.'" insists Gi Gi. When the boys and girls dance to that one many of them sneak into the kitchen to have a smooching session. I missed out on that. I'm kind of glad I did because they looked like they were doing more than just smooching. Their was a lot of grabbing going around. Jim Bob was grabbing Marj, Jon was grabbin' KP, and Harry was grabbin' Bev. Lump was grabbin' Rufus. It was a regular free for all. I saw the boys touching tits, butts and thighs.

I whisper to Gigi, "Never gonna let any boy do that." She nods and blushes. We feel a little like peeping toms.

I did wonder what it felt like though. Gigi looked like she was wondering too.

19

The Tornado

Life is like a tornado. It tears you up. Whirls you around. Slam dunks you down and you're never the same again. That happened to my brother, Jon. Mom comes into the front room and calmly takes Jon into the kitchen to talk to him privately. I have big ears so I hear what I'm not supposed to.

"Son, I just got off the phone with Doc Hudson. I'm afraid that your best friend Johnny is very ill. He was just diagnosised with having Tuberculosis. The family can'nt afford to send him to a recovery home so only prayer can help him."

"What's Tuberculosis and how did he get it? What can we do to help.?" asks a very concerned Jon E.

"Remember those TB tests you took at school 3 days ago. Well Johnny tested positive. They say his whole upper arm was nothing but red blisters." Tuberculosis is very contagious and dangerous. Sometimes its called Pulmonary Tuberculosis. That means it can destroy his lungs and immune system. Doc said he already has a bloody mucus when he coughs.

It could spread fast to his lymph nodes. But don't give up on him. Doc is giving him some medicine to combat these symptoms."

"Can I go see him. He's got to be scared."

"Remember how our house was quarantined when your sister had polio. Well the Tankers house is quarantined now. According to the Doctor it will be for two weeks. So no, you can not go see him for awhile. But you could send him notes. You can write him a get well card tonight and put it under their door in the morning. I know Johnny would love to get cards." Brother goes immediately to his room and stays there. He doesn't even come out for supper. I bring him my best writing paper and ink pen. He grunts a thank you and shuts his door.

That night while I was in the restroom I heard Jon E. trying to sell his soul to God in order to save Johnny. The wall is thin between brother's room and the restroom. I hear him talking to God.

"I'll become a preacher for you God. You know I'm a good speaker. I'll give all my worldly goods away to the poor. I don't have much but there are plenty who have less. I could study to become a doctor and maybe even find a cure for TB. I could try to save people. Would you like that? I'll do whatever you want me to God...just save Johnny. He is my best friend. He's a much better person than I am. You could take me instead of him." prays Jon E. The pleading went on and on until I finally hear an "Amen."

I go cry in my pillow thinking brother has sold his soul to God. At least it wasn't to the Devil I reason. Johnny was my secret of secrets boyfriend but I knew you couldn't bargain with God. If its your time to go you're going to go.

I get down on my knees beside my bed to pray. "God... please don't let Johnny suffer too much. He really is the best person there every was. Please take him to heaven and look after him. And please don't take brother even though he has asked you to. In Jesus' name Ahem," I add.

After the two weeks were up Jon E. visited Johnny faithfully everyday. He said Johnny had to wear a mask over his mouth so he wouldn't spread the TB germs. Jon E. loved Johnny like he was the brother he never had.

They had done everything together. But Johnny went down fast. There was extreme weight loss and blurred vision. When Johnny couldn't read anymore Jon E. read him the few get well cards that came for him.

"Johnny's starting to turn yellow looking and is as frail as an old man." informs brother crying as he tells Mom the news.

"I'm afraid that means he has jaundice. That means he's near the end," warns Mom as she pulls brother into a comforting hug. She was right. Preachers came and said prayers over Johnny's frail body. Willa Mae looks so sad at school.

"Willa Mae how is Johnny holding up?" I ask.

"He is at peace, and he received Jesus as his savior last night when the preacher was praying over him." she states. "He says he wants to go see God." But Lu Ann...I don't want him to go yet!"

I hug her to my breast and we cry together. He died on a beautiful spring day full of bird song and other signs of life. It felt like a piece of life had been ripped out of the very fabric of time. My heart ached for my brother, Jon E. He lost his best friend and his belief in God that day. I tried to tell him God was being merciful and taking Johnny's pain away. But Jon E. didn't want to hear any of that crap he said. He was one of the pallbearers at the funeral. Brother said the casket was so light he could have carried it by himself. That emotional tornado had ripped his soul apart and shredded his faith. I wonder if he will ever be the same?

Later that same year we had a real tornado touch down in River City. I was taking a timed test in typing class when what sounded like a freight train roared over the high school.

"Get down under your desks, yells Mrs. Cryder, the typing and shorthand teacher. "That sounds just like a tornado!"

I refuse the command because my passing typing depends on the results of this last speed test. I guess the adrenalin kicked in because I did pass the test. The lights had blinked but they didn't go out...thank goodness!

"A tornado did touch down in River City. There's an all clear now but its been reported that the roof was ripped off the school gym down at the end of Lowell Street" announces Principle Severs over the intercom system. This is the same man that my mom had once dated and actually been in love with before he went to college. Now that's according to her girlfriend Wren. Mom never told me that. I do wonder what I would look like if he were my Daddy. I bet I would be taller. He is giant tall as is both of his sons. He meet his sweet wife while going to college. With his girth I think she likes to cook and he likes to eat. She must be a real good cook.

According to my friend Rufus, "The way to a man's heart is through his stomach." Rufus's real name is Ruthie but almost everyone in River City has a nickname except for me. Rufus looks a little like her pet Cocker Spaniel with her pleading big eyes so maybe that's how she got a dog's nickname. If that's so about getting a man forget it. I'm not a good cook and really don't give a "doodly squat" about learning how. My girlfriend KP is taking homemaking in high school, but not me. KP is my girlfriend Kerry. I guess she has a lot of duty's thus that nickname. I'd rather take Latin. It least you get to use your mind instead of your taste buds. My favorite teacher, Mrs. Adele Lee, is the Latin teacher. She achieved some notoriety by marrying one of her students after he graduated. We go to home room and Skeeter's young sister Little Bit passes me a note. Its a petition to get Mrs. Lee fired because she had given her a F in English. I give Little Bit a furious look and just tear it up into tiny bits.

"If you ever try that again," I tell Little Bit, "you are going to live a life of pain" Then I show her a knuckle sandwich. She got the message and scurried away.

"You should try studying sometime if you want to pass," I yell at her fleeing backside. The bell rings for dismissal and I rush home to see if our house is still standing. A large limb from the pecan tree has crashed over the back porch. "Mama", I yell. Are you under there? Are you alive." Fear is like a choking hand stealing my breath away. I feel a hand on my shoulder and turn around. Its Mama! I can breathe again and take a quick gasp.

"I took shelter in Grandma's basement since we don't have any thing but a crawl space.' She notices I'm trembling and gives me a hug. For once I don't mind this public display of emotion and I could care less about up holding my tomboy reputation.

"I'm fine Pumpkin. I'm just happy to see you kids are OK. The storm has passed so lets go inside the house and light up some kerosene lanterns and some candles so we can have a source of light before it gets too dark. I don't know how long it will take to restore electricity." We carefully avoid downed telephone and electrical lines as we head into the house. "We can pretend we're a pioneer family" says Mom trying to cheer us up.

"We have plenty of coal for the coal stove." announces Jon E. I'll gather up some limbs and let them dry out on the back-porch just to be safe." He's pretending to be the man in the family until Dad gets home. He's doing a pretty good job of it considering he's my brother. I wonder if any of my friend's homes or families are hurt? I think maybe I'm a worry wart. When Dad gets home he is surprised by all the damage in the backyard. We eat by candle light. It makes everyone look kind of soft around the edges. I think Dad is getting romantic thoughts the way he is looking at Mom. I wake up in the middle of the night hearing creaking metal like a sewer cover sliding off a sewer except we don't have any sewers on Lowell street. I have no idea what it is but I hear moaning like a ghost and get frozen with fear. It could be our lost pet alligator coming out of the sewer seeking revenge. Unfortunately my wild imagination is scaring the shit out of me. Finally the squeaking and moaning stop and I go back to sleep. The next morning is Saturday and the whole family walks down to the tornado damaged gym to see if we can help clean up. The metal roof looks like a giant has ripped it off, crinkled it up and gleefully stomped on it.

"I don't want you kids going into the gym until structural damage is assessed, commands Dad. I'm going to go talk to the fire marshal."

We wait until Dad signals us over.

"The foundation is sound so while we men put tarp over the ripped off roof you kids run and get some old towels and gather up the basketball team and any other school kids willing to help. You need to dry off the gym floor before it buckles. We can't afford to be replacing it too."

We all work at saving the gym. Mom goes in and gathers up the soaked basketball uniforms and girl's gym suits to give them a washing. I was all for letting the gym suits rot.

Brother sitting on ripped of gym roof.

Lu Ann next to torando damage.

20

Music, Music, Music

The Teresa Brewer recording "Music, Music, Music" could be my mantra for my high school years.

"What do you want to be when you grow up?" asks Mom one breakfast near the end of my Junior Year.

"All I want is music, music, music!" I quip. I've decided that I wanted to go to college like my brother. "I want to go to Southern Illinois University. I could major in sports or music or even writing."

"Go to college? Girls don't go to college! Girls can become secretaries or nurses or even work in a store but they don't go to college. Besides we can't afford to help you."

"Jon isn't getting any help from you.. He got a scholarship to pay his way."

"We send him care packages of food and have bought him three new pairs of jeans. He earns expense money by working on campus."

"Well, I've got good grades. I bet I can get a scholarship too. And I'm a hard worker. I could get a campus job."

"We'll see what your Dad says about that but don't get your hopes up." warns Mom.

Much to Mom's surprise Dad tells me to go for it. So I kuckle down a little more seriously with my grades and my music. The Congregation Church's Ladies Aide must have gotten wind of my desire. They gather up money to send me to Summer Music Camp in Duqoin, IL. "All we ask is that you give a report to us of what you learn and experience," informs Mrs. Huddleson, the president of the club.

It's my last day of music camp and I decide I better start writing my report for my benefactors. I reference my class schedule to jog my memory. My roommate in the girls dorm is a flute player named Julie Harper. She is very nice but very serious. She's an extremely good musician. I love hearing her practice her flute as I write. It sounds like a bird is twittering around in the room.

My schedule states that I have breakfast at 7:30 to 8:30 then choir at 9 to 10 am. Piano ensemble at 11 to 12 pm. lunch at 12:30 to 1:30 Class piano improvisation from 2 to 3 pm and private piano from 3:30 to 4:30 and private voice from 4:45 to 5:15 then supper 5:30 to 6:30. OK I'll start with my first choir rehearsal. Director hands out a modern group of songs called "Frostiana" based on the poems of Robert Frost. That should impress them," I mumble as I write. The director's hands seemed to paint pictures in the air they were so descriptive.

"Sure wish I could learn to direct like him," I mumble.

"Second class consisted of 15 pianos playing light classical music at the same time. It was like a piano orchestra!

"That was so much fun but harder to stay together than I ever imaged," I contemplate outloud.

"Third class piano improvisation was the first time I'd ever played Dave Brubeck style. I didn't even know who Dave Brubeck was when the instructor mentioned him. When I took my licks (that's jazz talk for solo) I was too scared to jam too far from the base chord so I wasn't very impressive. I add a personal note.

"I think I'll ask Mrs. Brody to teach me some music theory. I didn't understand doodly squat about diminished 7ths or major 9th chords or even what they meant about a one chord in the second position, "I mumble.

"What are you mumbling about?" asks my roommate, Julie.

"I'm just writing my report to my benefactors. All they want to know is that they haven't wasted their money by sending me to this camp.

"I don't know about you but I've learned so much it makes my head spin," comments Julie.

"Oh, I totally agree." I say as I return to my writing.

Fourth class is private piano lessens. My teacher is from the SIU college piano faculty. Dr. Tinker, my teacher, looks just like Alfred Hitchcock, that scary movie writer. I was nervous enough without him looking so spooky. He is a large man with big hands. He's a Johann Sebastian Bach fanatic so you can guess what music I had to play. I had no idea Bach wrote so many sonatas! The book I had to purchase is as heavy as a brick!" You have to have a very exacting and an almost analytical mind to play Bach. Its an entirely new experience for me.

"Fifth class is private voice lessons. My teacher is a female and I can tell shes' kind of disappointed in the lack of strength in my voice. I wish Rufus were here to take my place. She would have impressed her.

"You need to breath from your diaphragm not your chest young lady she admonishes me. You don't breath right."

I didn't know you breath different to sing. I thought breathing was just a natural thing. Boy, was I wrong. By the end of the lessons I could sing a longer phrase without sneaking a breath and I was a little louder. On the sixth day of camp we practiced for final day concert. On the seventh day the gala concert was given at 6 pm. Mrs. Huddleson drove up with Mrs. Brody and my Mom to hear the evening concert and take me home. Even I was impressed by the different musical ensembles performances. Choral, Piano, Instrumental and then all of it together with the song "Ode to Joy" by Beethoven. I got chills singing that last number with the whole ensemble. What a wonderful summer it has been.

"Thank you, thank you so much Ladies Aid!"

The summer ends and I resume my high school chorus and contest solo accompaniment. Much to my surprise the music teacher asks me to sing in a quartet. Rufus sang lead and I sang alto. Cathy and KP were also in the quartet. We went to state music contest with "Down By the Riverside" and actually won a ribbon. Mom made all our costume dresses. They were a polished pale blue cotton, full in the skirt and a little too low necked for me. At the same contest I played Rachmaninov's Prelude in G Minor for my piano contest piece. My hands ached because I really have too small of a paw to play his music. But I did it. I'm part bulldog my Dad says. Rachmaninov wrote his music for his own big hands. I made the mistake of glancing out into the audience right before the end and I saw Mom. The surprise of seeing her threw me completely off and I had to stop to remember the correct ending. I was so embrassed. The judges just smiled understandingly and to my suprise gave me a 1st place. They told me I would have gotten a Superior rating if I hadn't stopped. The year before I had played one of my favorite pieces "The Rustle of Spring Op. 32 #3 by the Norwegian composer C. Sinding and gotten a first place. I had so hoped to get a Superior this year. Oh well, that's life. When I accompanied the high school production of the musical "Annie Laurie" my brother sang in a quartet and wore kilts. He sure looked funny with his knobby knees showing. To my surprise the guys in the quartet did a great job! My up the street neighbor boy Lump Stevens sang the lead. He has a drop dead gorgeous voice that just seemed to rumble out of his chest. Rufus, who had the girl lead, and he were supposed to kiss on stage. The whole cast was laying bets on how long they would hold the kiss. I put a quarter in for a 3 second kiss knowing how shy Lump was. I had to stand on the piano bench to see and time it. Boy was I wrong. Lump and Rufus held it 15 seconds! Skeeter won the bet. I was so surprised I didn't get down from the bench in time to play the intro to their last song. By the time I got it together they were singing in one key and I was playing in another. So I just stopped and they winged it on their own to the end and great applause. Rufus confronts me after the show.

"Where were you Lou Ann? Did you go out for coffee or something!" She was mad cap angry.

"Hey, how was I to know Lump was going to get all love sick on stage. I'm surprised you could even sing after that kiss!" I tease.

"Yeah that was some kiss", Rufus admits with a blush. Thinking about the kiss got her out of her hornet mad mood..thank goodness!

Brother, with his knobby knees, and the rest of the cast
of the high school musical, Annie Laurie

21

Phoenix from the Ashes

"Gee sis you look like a fright night at a Frankenstein movie." Why were you so serious?" teases Jon E. as he looks at my Senior pictures I had just brought home to show the folks. He is home from college for a weekend visit and is his usual un-charming self.

"My new perm was so tight it made my brains hurt." I quiped. I think the pictures make me look distinguised though."

"I agree," says Dad. She is a handsome young women in these proofs. Quit teasing your sister Jon E. Your a man now."

Jon E. looks a little embrassed and I blush from Dad's calling me handsome.

"Sorry Sis I was just teasing. They are good pictures."

I almost faint in surprise. A first has occured. Jon E. saying sorry. Maybe he is growing up? I wonder?

"When do you come up for Freshman Orientation Sis?

"Jerri Winegardner and I are going up together on the bus Saturday morning. I didn't even know she wanted to go to college.

"Is KP going to college?" asks brother.

"She wants to but needs to build up her bank roll before she can even think about it."

"How about your friend Rufus?"

"She has applied for a music scholorship at Champaign, IL I expect her to get it. She has such an outstanding voice. How is Lump doing in college? I know he got a music scholarship to SIU, Carbondale."

"He is having a rough time with his math class but I'm helping him and I think he'll pass. He has an almost operatic voice so they love him in the music department. He has gotten the lead in the summer production of Brigadoon. I'm going to be in it too so I'm hoping the family can come up and see it."

"Can we Mom? I'd really love to see a live college musical."

"I don't see why not. How about it Ben?"

"Sure hon I wouldn't miss it for the world."

I think about how all my classmates will be going so many different places and ways. I wonder if it will ever be the same. Saturday comes and Jerri and I get on the Greyhound Bus to go to the University. Jerri and I naturally sit together. We are both so excited about exploring the campus. The bus trip is long and boring so we get to exchanging gossip.

"Did you hear about the Chinese fire drill they had in Mudville last Monday? Jerri asks.

"What do you mean by Chinese fire drill?" I reply.

"Well, this is how it went down according to my older brother who drives a delivery truck in Mudville. A derelict building was being knocked down that was right next to a bakery. The not so bright workmen tried to knock down the bricks from the bottom first instead of the top. One hit and the whole wall collapsed on top of the next door bakery and started a fire."

"I still don't get it. Why was it a Chinese fire drill?"

"Just wait I haven't finished yet. They had a brand new fire truck and proudly drove it, bells clanging, to the fireplug that just happened to be directly in front of the burning bakery."

"So they put out the fire right?"

"Wait now; it gets better. They tightly attach the hose to the fireplug.

"Yes, of course; so what?"

"A spark from the fire lands in the front seat of the fire truck and catches it on fire."

"Oh my gosh no!" I say as I start laughing.

"The volunteer firemen get so excited they drive away full throttle." But...and there is a long pause."

"Oh lordy don't keep me in suspense!" By that time I was hysterical.

"They forgot to unattach the fire hose. The fireplug was yanked out of the ground spewing like Old Faithful, the upholstery of the firetruck went up in flames, and both buildings burn completely down. Now that's why I said it was a Chinese fire drill."

Laughing too hard to answer I nod my head in total agreement. We finally arrive on campus and are shown around. Old Main looks so old and distinguished. Even the bricks on the steps are worn down from the ghosts of students past. As we board the bus for the boring trip back home, I wrack my brain trying to come up with something to top Jerri's funny Chinese fire drill story. Then I remember the story that was told at Brody's Drug Store as I worked at the soda fountain last week.

"Did you hear about the Volkswagen trying to gun down Dover's truck last week?" I ask Jerri.

"No, what happend?" asked a surprised Jerri.

"Well... while zipping out of a parking spot Dover notices a Volkswagon tailgating him so closely it was eating his exhaust. He thought maybe it was robbers trying to run him off the road. He had just picked up his tavern take and was going to deposit it in the bank."

"Oh my gosh, did he get away."

"No, he couldn't shake it so he decided to drive right up the the police station."

"Smart move," says Jerri then she sees my smile.

"Ok what's the punch line?" she asks.

"It was a punch alright. Dover slammed on his brakes and the Volkswagon punched past him and slammed into the jailhouse."

"Did they get the robbers?"

"There were no robbers. There was no one in the car. It seems like the Volkswagon's side mirror had become attached to the truck's tailgate.

"Oh my gosh, that is too funny," says Jerri snorting as she laughs.

"It was whizzing along attached because Dover had cut too close to it when he pulled out. So now Dover owes the jailhouse for repairs and the surprised owner for damages. You could call that story 'The chase of the fathom robbers'."

We are both laughing as we step off the bus in River City and are greeted by friends and family. Our school friends tease us by saying, "Well at least we know it wasn't you two who burned down the school."

"What are you talking about." Jerri and I ask looking at each other then at them like they are out of their gourds.

"And that's not a good joke to make about the school burning down, scolds Jerri.

"But its no joke! It did burn down, informs Curley.

"What", scream Jerri and I at the same time. Ellie May, our high school principle's youngest, tells us, with tears in her eyes, about watching it burn down. Then Jerri's folks drive up and we say our goodbyes. My parents walk me home and I learn more about the disaster as we go.

"It seems the fire started in the basement. The fire marshal thinks the furnace over heated and exploded." informs Dad. It was an old furnace."

"We still have a month of school to finish. Where will we go? Will we have to go all the way to Karo by bus to their high school?" I was dreading that possibility because we had always been school basketball rivals. The basketball team once teepeed their high school after one of our wins.

"Don't worry, the Methodist Church and the Congregation Church have opened up their facilities so you will go there to finish up your school year." informs Mom.

Will they ever rebuild the school I wonder thinking of all the fond memories I have had going there?

Dad smiles and says, "Principal Lee and I called for an emergency school board meeting. The school board was forced to face financial reality so consolidation is finally coming to River City. I didn't think I'd live to see the day. They will build a school for both black and white students out in the country. It will be better equiped and brand new. So, "Out of the ashes shall rise the Phoenix" quotes Dad sounding very scholarly.

"Graduation will be held in the gym. But yours will be the last class to graduate from River City High," informs Mom.

I comment proudly, "I am so proud of you and Mr. Lee, Dad!"

Finally an unsegregated school system! "In a bittersweet moment I think of Charlie and Easter and wonder what they could have achieved if it had come sooner. As you know...wondering is what I do best. "You know Dad. I can hardly wait to go to college where blacks and whites, reds and yellows are all brothers and sisters under the skin and as such are there to live and learn together."

"I know just what you mean Pumpkin. Prejudice runs deep in the South. It's just like old man river. It flows deep in the dark, frightened part of men's mean spirited souls. I think we need a soul searching flood to cleanse this land of this racist blight on the land."

"I hope it comes before its too late." pipes up Jon E.

"I'm tired of this nations KKK mentality. I've already started protest sit-ins on campus."

For once I totally agree with brother and give him a thumbs up sign because he's right. It just isn't fair. Such thoughts and feelings all started when I was just a blustering tomboy. I smile thinking... some parts of me will never change. It's in my nature to always tilt at unfair windmills. Just like my Dad. (and brother)

Lu Ann's hig school graduation picture.

THE END

Printed in the United States
By Bookmasters